Lariba

A NOVEL BY **LOUIS SHEPPARD**

Lariba

A NOVEL BY **LOUIS SHEPPARD**

2nd Edition

University Press Plc
R.C. 25783
...the foremost publishers

FOR INFORMATION CONTACT:
University Press Plc
IBADAN ABA ABEOKUTA ABUJA AJAH AJEGUNLE AKURE BENIN
IKEJA IKORODU ILORIN IJEBU-ODE JOS KADUNA KANO MAKURDI
MINNA ONITSHA OSOGBO OWERRI PORT HARCOURT WARRI ZARIA

2nd Edition Cover design by Michaela Licorish with DreamEmpire Publishing
2nd Edition Edit & Book interior design by Joyce Licorish with DreamEmpire Publishing

ISBNS:
Paperback: 978 978 940 579 4
KDP Hardback: 979 883 606 696 3
INGRAM SPARK Hardback 979-8-9908583-3-6

First Edition: Mar 2021
Second Edition: June 2023

Published by University Press PLC
Three Crowns Building, Jericho, P.M.B. 5095, Ibadan, Nigeria
E-mail: unipress@universitypressplc.com | Website: www.universitypressplc.com
0802 342 1333, 0802 052 1801, 0802 052 1802, 0802 052 1807
Toll Free: 0800 877 5264
in Association with DreamEmpire Publishing | Duluth, GA 30096

STAY CONNECTED:

www.facebook.com/upplc
www.twitter.com/upplc
www.linkedin.com/in/upplc
www.youtube.com/upplc

DEDICATION

For my brother, Michael Sheppard, who I love with all my being. I will always keep in my heart his perseverance, forgiving spirit, warmth and caring ways. He was and ALWAYS will be a giant MY HERO.

ACKNOWLEDGEMENTS

CHARITY BEGINS AT HOME. For me, that means Paulina Amoah, and Jessica Otiwah Ansah. Without them, I would still be conducting revisions on this writing project.

I am indebted to a host of professionals who influenced my concepts. Among them are Kwame Essuman (Ghana Airport Ltd.), Joseph Atayem Awantungo, Edmond Ewool, and Shalon Potts. For editorial assistance, I am indebted to Melva J. Davis who, with great care and thoroughness, plowed through the many changes in the manuscript and added the finishing touch to an otherwise unpolished gem.

The publishing advice of Janice Pemida, her guidance, support and, most important, her patience was invaluable. Lastly, I want to express my gratitude to Cassandra Larkai, Seraphine Asem, Elizabeth Tutuwass Boafo, Ericka Gene Littleton, and Dereka D. Byars, who volunteered and read the manuscript in its infancy and offered valuable commentary and insight.

This book is a tribute to their honesty.

FOREWORD

FOR A MAN TO KNOW HIS FUTURE, HE MUST SEARCH A LIFETIME FOR HIS PAST. This book is a testimony to how important life's journey must become for every individual. I am considered by some a BLACK man, others an African American man, and then there are others who use a language that is much harsher to describe me, as three-fifths of a human. For me, I was in search of MAN. My longing to determine and develop the man I needed to become led me to begin my travels to the Motherland, Our Home, as we know Home, here on earth. My soul was restless … in search of the HUMAN…within the depths of my soul … AFRICA became my refuge, my peace, my pain, my joy, my LOVE, my sheer being. Mother Africa served to define ME, an African in America.

My travels began with tours throughout the Motherland, inquisitive, curious and, yet, with a longing to find home. As an educator, a parent, we learn how important experiences in life play such a vital role in assisting children to respect and understand the world in which we live. However, we find ourselves so enslaved within our collective societies working to amass wealth, that we often find ourselves empty inside, wondering how life missed us.

In discovering the true beauty of HISTORY and not His Story, I have found solace in discovering my own being. I share Lariba with you as my contribution of finding oneself through the art of expressing love, pain, joy, disappointment, death, birth, human relationships, and life.

Come travel with me through Lariba.

Enjoy the ride.

Melva J. Davis
Melva Davis School of Academic Excellence
Victorville, California

INTRODUCTION

"The prerequisite for writing is to have something to say."

– Langston Hughes

THE SMALL, MALNOURISHED, bow-legged girl was happy despite the pebbles, sharp stones, and horse manure that covered the unpaved road she walked every day. With a smile on her face, she greeted everyone, young and old, respectfully, while gracefully skipping down the road and occasionally humming her favorite melody. The hummingbirds fluttered their wings happily, enjoying the melodies carried by the wind created by the girl's rhythmic skipping.

Despite her sketchy and farfetched dreams, the small girl believed that one day her life would be different.

Hailing from the Upper East Region of Ghana, the girl's upbringing was a tapestry woven with resilience, courage, and fortitude. As a young woman, she possessed striking beauty, but her life was torn between two remarkable individuals. One led a dramatic life with boundless potential, while the other steadily climbed the ladder of success, accumulating accolades and promotions.

Both were loving, handsome, and protective, making them ideal husband material. Their lives provided a rollercoaster of drama, suspense, and tragedy worth experiencing again.

Louis Sheppard

PROLOGUE

DARK CLOUDS HOVERED HIGH above the gray northern skies. Clouds pregnant with water ready to burst free. The season was changing. Thunderstorms were fast approaching. Soon, rainfall would nourish the fields and feed the livestock. Adventurous times for an eight-year-old village girl named Lariba. Lariba slept next to her mother on a bamboo mat in the village. During the night, she felt an itch on her leg and instinctively scratched. Moments later, the itch was closer to her thigh, and she scratched again vigorously. The itch went away. She turned slightly towards her mother and went back to sleep undisturbed for the rest of the night. The following day, she awoke well-rested, rubbed her eyes, and yawned with outstretched arms. Then she noticed something crawling on her arm – a black scorpion.

She screamed, "Momma!" She ran out of the room hysterically in a flash, arms flailing. She stumbled and fell to the ground. The scorpion was moving, crawling up her shoulder, onto her neck, and into her thick hair. Lariba was beyond frantic; she was screaming and yelling for her mother. She could feel the scorpion crawling in her hair. Her brother saw and heard the commotion; Lariba rolling on the ground was comical. At first, he laughed, but then he saw a scorpion crawling in her hair.

Black scorpions are common in the village but no less dangerous. From a scorpion bite, with the adrenalin rush of the victim, the venom moves quickly throughout the body and can be lethal almost immediately. Lariba was petrified. Eventually, the scorpion became disentangled from her hair. Hysterically, Lariba scrambled to her feet and ran as fast as she could, getting away from the scorpion. The scorpion crawled to a hiding space with long outstretched legs, but her mother crushed it underfoot into the dust. 'I got it, Lariba, don't cry.'

But Lariba continued to cry uncontrollably in her mother's arms. 'You okay, Lariba?' her brother asked, with a smirk on his face. To him, it was funny seeing his sister rolling on the ground, screaming and yelling. But for Lariba, it was a frightening experience, something she prayed never to encounter again. It took a while before her mother was able to calm her down. From that day forward, Lariba feared bugs, insects, and reptiles. Akurugo, her mother, became her first heroine.

CONTENTS

CHAPTER 1

SUBRUNGO

Sumbrungo was a small farming village in the Upper East Region of Ghana. A village filled with guinea fowls, dogs, sheep, goats, and cows. The village was commonly referred to as "dry land" or a desert when it didn't rain. The rainy season could last several months. When it did rain, people got extremely excited, because rain brings about the sowing of crops, which in turn gives a good harvest. Cows, goats, and sheep welcomed the rainy season because there would be plenty of fresh green grass to graze.

Regardless of weather conditions, Saturday mornings were always a day of cleaning and cooking in the village of Sumbrungo. Lariba was enthusiastic about house chores from an early age; mimicking her mother's daily activities, she enjoyed cooking and cleaning.

She had remarkable strength and endurance and would cheerfully go about her Saturday activities in good spirits. Scrubbing bathrooms and mopping the entire house before the crack of dawn was soothing for her.

Saturday mornings were spent washing clothes. Lariba would fill the basin with fresh water, pour a cup of detergent, straddle the rubber basin, and commence to scrub. When the water slowly turned a brownish color, it was evident that the dirt had stubbornly separated from the clothes. After a vigorous wash, the clothes were ready for the clothesline. Lariba lugged the rubber basin full of damp clothes outside, where she carefully stood on tiptoes to reach the clothesline and pin the clothes to the string.

On Saturday mornings, Lariba was always in high spirits and eager to chat with her best friend, her mother, Akurugo. Lariba sang alongside her mother while she worked in her colorful handmade bonnet woven by her mother.

Akurugo was a mother of five, with Lariba as her youngest. Dark-skinned, she was of slender build and very attractive. Daily, Akurugo received praise from villagers – both male and female – for her beauty. She was admired by people in the village, including the elders and chiefs, not only because she was beautiful but also because she was a good mother, a great cook, and a hard worker. Akurugo committed everything to memory; she never wrote down the ingredients or used a measuring cup when she prepared food, nor did she share her recipes. Lariba learned how to prepare food by watching her mother in the kitchen. Rice balls with groundnut soup were her specialty. Next to her mother, Lariba was considered the best cook in the entire compound.

Her father, Baba Atuonah, was the undisputed, God-fearing head of the household. In speech and manner, he possessed the leadership of the proud African warrior, beloved and revered by the villagers. Baba Atuonah was tall and handsome, his skin tone like fine brass. A man of few words, fearless and protective of his family, he believed the ancestors were guardian angels watching his every move. He felt accountable, knowing he would be held responsible for his good deeds and misdeeds one day. "Give everything to God" was Baba Atuonah's favorite words of wisdom. Because of that, most people called him All Mighty. Lariba revered her Baba; always seeking his approval. Baba was a great storyteller. In the darkness of the night, with only the moonlight, he would gather the children of the village and tell stories. Baba was a fantastic storyteller!

Baba knew his children well, especially Lariba, who was inquisitive and sometimes stubborn. Her curious nature allowed her to shadow and learn quickly from Akurugo. At an early age, Lariba was impatient and easy to anger. Baba was a wise man and had patience. Baba often reminded Lariba, 'Never let someone else decide when you get angry.'

Akurugo and Baba Atuonah were loving parents who struggled mightily to feed five children. Baba Atuonah was a village farmer. He planted and harvested okra, garden egg, pepper, and tomato seeds. With his mighty hoe handed down to him from his grandfather, Baba Atuonah dug yam from the ground. He fed the chicken and the cattle and managed the livestock.

His wife, Akurugo, sold yam, pineapple, dried fish, watermelon, and orange along the roadside. Akurugo and Baba Atuonah's earnings were barely enough to feed and sustain a family of five.

The oldest child, Agnes, had moved to the city to attend nursing school. The only recollection Lariba had of her big sister, Agnes, was when she left the house one early morning carrying two suitcases and walking to a taxi at the roadside. It was a painful experience for Lariba and a sad day for the entire family.

There were many activities during the night in the Northern Region. People from the village gathered together, and the elders told stories. Funerals and funeral rites were conducted during the night. Marriage ceremonies were also performed during the night.

School was tough in the village, with no electricity. They worked in open classrooms. Children defecated in the bushes. They dug holes in the ground with their hands. Boys and girls used writing papers and leaves to wipe themselves. Boys urinated on the roadside; girls squatted in the bush. These were common practices for boys and girls up to age 11. There were no toilets, no urinals. There were just open bathhouses. They simply defecated in the open!

She and the other children walked barefoot. There were neither beds nor mattresses. People slept on woven straw mats. What Lariba and the other children of the village feared more than anything else was the night. Without electricity, there was pitch-black darkness. The only light was the moonlight. Children ate lizards, hunted snakes, and climbed trees for birds for fun. Baba and Akurugo, Lariba's parents, worked hard to make way for their children.

LARIBA'S FAVORITE pastime was swimming in the "forbidden river." Playing in the river was forbidden by both Akurugo and Baba Atuonah. Lariba would sneak off at night to swim in the dark, murky water. 'The river is full of water snakes and gigantic toads with short, squat bodies and very long hind legs for leaping; they are big enough to jump on you and swallow you,' Baba would tell this tale to the children, trying to frighten them. Despite repeated warnings from Akurugo and Baba, the river was fun and exciting for the children of the village. Occasionally, Lariba would catch a fish with her bare hands. When it happened, it was the reason for the children to celebrate; they celebrated often. Lariba's first catch came when a small undersized fish swam close to her legs in the shallow end of the river. She literally reached down and snatched the slimy prize from the water and triumphantly raised the poor squirming fish in the air. As she proudly raised the fish in the air, she suddenly felt the river bottom shift beneath her feet. She lost her footing and fell face-first into the river. Fish still in hand, she panicked.

'Help! Help!' she cried, gasping for air and swallowing gulps of river water. The river's bottom became quicksand taking command and swallowing her skinny legs. Because she was always the youngest of the bunch, the other children kept a watchful eye on her. The other children swam to her rescue when she slipped into the river. Fortunately for Lariba, Kwame, who lived in the village across the road, occasionally played in the river with the other children. He was an unofficial lifeguard and an excellent swimmer. Kwame heard the screams of desperation and swam to the rescue. He effortlessly pulled the girl to safety. Lying on her back at the river's edge, out of breath and gasping for air, she slowly calmed down. Kwame was a lifesaver. Surprisingly, she still managed to hold her fish. It was her first catch and a risky catch at that. Only after the deadly river experience nearly took her young life, she fully understood Baba's words of wisdom. Lariba and the others decided to celebrate privately away from home. They secretly held a fish fry at Kwame's house to celebrate the only fish caught at the river. She sneaked back into the house undetected and fell asleep. She was exhausted by the river experience.

At daybreak, after the deadly river experience, a slight breeze gently grazed her face. She woke up, arms outstretched, smiling from an eventful night. In the distance, she could hear the crowing of the roosters and the goats milling about in the compound. She turned and looked up into the heavens and saw gray skies. In the village, this was nature's way of forecasting rain. She slowly sat upright, rubbing her eyes. Gracefully, she sidestepped the chickens and pigs wandering through the compound, searching for food. She noticed the tree in the compound swaying from the gentle breeze. The tree branches swayed unnaturally as though being nibbled by a hungry goat standing high on its hind legs. But it was not a goat. Lariba noticed an unfamiliar woman picking leaves from the tree and placing the leaves in a small plastic bag. Who is this strange person in her house picking leaves from her tree? she wondered. Lariba couldn't see the woman's face as her back was turned. Curious, she moved closer. The woman turned slightly and faced her. She stared unblinkingly at the woman; her identity registered in her consciousness. She stared at the woman's jet-black curly hair and discovered who she was – Agnes, her elder sister. If anyone had later asked her to repeat her sister's initial words, she would not have been able to do so. 'Agnes,' she screamed. She ran and leaped into her big sister's outstretched arms.

Tears of joy streamed down her face. Lariba had not seen her big sister in years and often cried herself to sleep almost every night since she left. But now, Agnes was back, picking leaves from the family tree. Lariba was happy!

Agnes stepped back to get a good look at her baby sister. She knew instinctively why her mother asked her to return to the village on short notice. Later her mother confessed that the entire village was sick, coughing and sneezing with a fever. There was sickness in the house, and she could see it when she looked into her baby sister's eyes. Even Lariba's friend, Kwame, was feverish. Malaria had gripped the village.

After greeting her baby sister, Agnes asked her to help pick a few more leaves from the tree. Akurugo and Baba Atuonah were getting older, and Baba suffered from borderline hypertension. Akurugo could keep his blood pressure stable when she prepared solo – a village brew prepared with hibiscus leaves, ginger, and guinea pepper boiled in hot water. The brew was effective in treating hypertension. But Baba refused to take the brew regularly, and his blood pressure spiraled out of control often. His hypertension even affected his vision. Only Akurugo knew how to prepare the bitter brew to his taste. In nursing school, Agnes learned how to treat hypertension through medicine prescribed by a physician, filled at a local pharmacy. But this modern medicine was costly and had many side effects. Agnes learned in nursing school that prescription drugs taken properly and regularly over time would effectively treat ailments, even hypertension. Still, she also knew that leaves plucked from a bitter leaf tree and boiled with ginger worked even better without side effects. Old school remedies and herbs practiced by village elders worked remarkably well.

CHAPTER 2

DUNGEONS

IT WAS THE END-OF-YEAR SCHOOL TRIP at the village school, and all sixty-five enrolled students were scheduled to attend. On the day of the trip, the school buzzed with excitement as children ran about, chatting and playing with friends. Parents and family stood nearby, happy to see their children excited about the trip that would be a memorable learning journey. Ms. Adongo, the faculty advisor, instructed the children to line up with their permission slips in hand, ready to board the run-down school bus. Assisting Ms. Adongo on the trip was one volunteer parent, Ms. Amoah.

Ms. Adongo and Ms. Amoah were the only two supervising adults responsible for the rambunctious group of sixty-five elementary school children. The children quickly lined up and settled down after being warned several times about excessive noise by Rev. Father Francis Adom, who was also the school headmaster. With his commanding tone, the children understood and found their seats, allowing Ms. Adongo to take roll call.

The bus ride to Cape Coast Castle and Elmina Castle, referred to as "Dungeons" by Ms. Adongo, was long and bumpy. The gravel roads were filled with sharp rocky potholes, and slow-moving traffic, as well as goats, sheep, and chickens, made the trip even longer. Despite the challenges, the children remained happy and excited to be on the trip.

Upon reaching Cape Coast, the students grew silent, eagerly gazing out the windows. Ms. Adongo, familiar with the area, served as both a tour guide and faculty advisor. She gathered the children's attention and gave them a brief overview of the history of Cape Coast Castle and Elmina Castle. The children listened attentively as they caught sight of the imposing white structures in the morning fog. Ms. Adongo declared their arrival and instructed them on how to exit the bus safely and stay with the group inside the castle.

The students disembarked and gathered around Ms. Adongo, who reminded them to stick together and ask questions during the tour. A museum educator named Kwesi introduced himself and explained that he would be their guide for Cape Coast Castle. He shared the history of the castle, highlighting the strategic location and the dangers it faced from rival European slave traders. Despite the dreadful history of the African Slave Trade, Kwesi's storytelling skills made the tour enjoyable for the students.

As they entered the Male Dungeon, Kwesi asked the students to turn off their cameras and electronic devices to fully experience the environment where captives were held for weeks at a time. The dungeon was dark, humid, and dreary, and the walls were lined with human skulls and figurines. The heat and discomfort made the students realize the harsh conditions the captives endured. Kwesi described the lack of light, fresh air, and sanitary conditions in the dungeon, painting a vivid picture of the suffering the captives went through.

Next, the group proceeded to the Female Dungeon, where Kwesi shared the horrors experienced by women and children held captive there. He pointed out the unsanitary conditions, lack of privacy, and the sexual abuse suffered by the captives. Lariba, one of the students, was deeply affected by the information and separated herself from the group to pray at a makeshift altar. She questioned why such inhumanity was allowed to happen and hoped for justice and answers from Rev. Father Francis Adom back in the village.

After the tour, Mr. Kwesi thanked the class for being attentive. "I hope you learned something today; please come again," he said.

A commotion erupted in the gift shop near the dungeon entrance as the children boarded the bus. Two non-African men dressed in foreign attire argued over the ownership of a carved wooden African doll—a doll resembling a slave girl with oversized lips, bare-breasted, and looped earrings. Lariba turned away in disgust.

"Hope you all enjoyed the Cape Coast Dungeon," said Ms. Adongo, the first time she openly referred to Cape Coast Castle as a dungeon. Lariba now understood and agreed. "Next stop, Elmina Castle."

Lariba couldn't bear another tour through a "castle." She pleaded with Ms. Adongo to cancel the visit to Elmina Castle. "Everybody is tired and hungry," she said. "How about we cancel this portion of the end-of-year school trip and return to school? We've had enough," she pleaded from the rear of the bus.

"We will only be at Elmina Castle briefly," assured Ms. Adongo. "It's just down the road, not far."

The bus proceeded to Elmina Castle. Upon arrival, Ms. Adongo directed the students to disembark carefully. "Watch your step, please."

Once inside Elmina Castle, Lariba distanced herself from the group and explored independently. The tour of Elmina Castle was brief, as promised by Ms. Adongo. Lariba rejoined the group just before they headed for the castle exit. As she followed, she noticed a plaque on the wall that captured her sentiments:

"In the everlasting memories of the anguish of our ancestors. May those who died Rest in Peace. May those who return find their roots. May humanity never again perpetrate such injustice against humanity. We the living vow to uphold this."

Hawkers flocked around the bus, hoping to sell food, trinkets, bracelets, and souvenirs. Exhausted, the children slowly boarded the bus, most only holding a bottle of water. The tour had been emotionally and physically draining. The bus fell into a deathly quiet state. No laughter or small chatter could be heard.

Some students fell fast asleep once they found their seats on the bus. Others stared out the window with somber faces, almost in a distant trance.

Lariba remained quiet. Tears rolled down her cheeks as her face rested against the window. She looked at the world and the people on the road with blurred vision. She shut her eyes and imagined herself frightened, defenseless, naked, and chained in the grip of merciless dungeon guards. Her body flinched in agony and pain from the sting of rawhide. Lariba longed to talk to Rev. Father Francis more than ever. But what would she say to him? What could he say to her? He had been to the dungeons before. He knew the history of the transatlantic slave trade.

The bus arrived back at the school almost at midnight. The school was dark and motionless. No parents awaited their return from the trip. The only voice heard when the school bus door opened was Rev. Father Francis Adom's.

"Welcome back! I hope you all had a good trip," said Rev. Father Francis Adom. "Thank God, you made it home safely." His eyes were fixed on Lariba's face. It was clear she wanted to speak, talk, share, and tell what she had seen, heard, and felt at Cape Coast and Elmina Castle.

Finally, she spoke. "I saw myself in the dungeons, Father. I saw other people, my ancestors, too. I felt tremendous sadness and suffering. It was real. It was a dungeon, not a castle. Human

beings, not savages, were held captive in those dungeons. Human beings chained together marched through the Door of No Return and boarded the slave ships," she declared. Lariba believed that Rev. Father Francis knew how she felt as he, too, had visited the dungeons many times. Lariba knew that Rev. Father Francis Adom was searching for words that would comfort her soul, but the words never came.

After nearly a two-mile walk at night with no parental guidance, Lariba reflected on what it must have been like to be kidnapped from the village, chained with strangers, barefoot, and marched on unpaved roads for miles. The experiences of the trip became real as she pondered. She had been properly educated. The children finally reached their village safe and sound.

It was Saturday morning, and Lariba was still sound asleep in the village. The compound was busy with guinea fowls, sheep, goats, and cows moving about. Agnes and Momma were preparing Baba's favorite meal of jollof rice with chicken and fish. Two days had passed, and Agnes was still in the village helping Momma with household chores and cooking.

Lariba's friend, Kwame, who lived just across the road, was ill. Lariba asked Agnes if she could go and visit, but Agnes emphatically said no.

"There is a strange sickness in the air; staying close to the village is best. Kwame will be fine soon," assured Agnes. "He will be up and about and chasing you around the compound before you know it. Let's just wait a while. Besides, we need to spend some time together. I haven't seen you since you were a small girl."

Lariba loved her big sister, who was like her mother. Days turned into weeks, and still, no word came from Kwame. Lariba was worried. She thought about sneaking across the road to visit her friend when Momma, Baba, and Agnes were asleep but feared she would be caught.

Aside from playing in the "forbidden river," Lariba's favorite pastime was chasing chickens in the compound. The chickens pecked for food and scraps most of the day, occasionally raising their heads and scattering when Lariba gave chase. They easily avoided her playful ambushes. However, when the chickens became annoyed, the fun quickly turned serious. The rooster, with its razor-sharp claws, would defend its flock. With wings flapping high in the air, the rooster would chase Lariba away on several occasions. On one occasion, as she playfully skipped away from the rooster, not paying attention, she ran into the compound gate and nearly knocked herself unconscious. The rooster descended on her ankles, drawing blood with its sharp claws. She now bore a scar on her ankle from the rooster's attack.

Village schools were grossly inadequate compared to city schools. They had limited budgets and lacked basic facilities like water tanks, resulting in thirsty students throughout the school day. Due to poor pay, there was a shortage of certified teachers. Many children sat on dirty floors as there was a scarcity of seats and desks. Open classrooms with no doors were common, and classroom furnishings were old and damaged. Each student had access to only two sheets of paper. Donated books from city schools were no longer in use, with missing or ripped-out pages. The school curriculum was minimal.

Rev. Father Francis Adom, the school headmaster, prioritized knowledge of scripture. Students were expected to know and recite biblical verses. Rev. Adom believed that knowing the Bible constituted a well-rounded education. In reality, city schools were more advanced compared to village schools.

Parental involvement was minimal as most parents had no formal education. Men in the village worked in the fields and tended to livestock to feed their families, while women sold clothes and prepared food to sell along the roadside.

In village life, grandparents and elders played a central role. They took in their grandchildren whose parents were working and living in the city. They were hard workers, but their efforts didn't yield much money at the end of the day.

Lariba didn't know who made the decision for her to move and live with her big sister in the city. What she did know was that Akurugo and Baba were getting older and unable to manage the compound efficiently or handle the mischievousness of the other children in the house. Clearly, Akurugo and Baba were in the final quarter of their life's journey with no remaining time-outs. They were tired. Agnes weighed her options on how best to help her aging parents.

CHAPTER 3

AGNES

MOVING TO THE CITY to live with her big sister, Agnes, her husband, Rex, and their two children had real advantages. Rex was a gentle man with a warm compromising spirit. As an active and popular local politician, Rex was often away from home for meetings and political gatherings. While Rex was the head of the family, Agnes assumed the role of "head of household." She assigned household chores to Lariba from the very first day she arrived.

Lariba's life revolved around housework. Despite her two nephews, one a year older and the other a year younger than her, living in the house, Lariba quickly took on the responsibility of washing, mopping, and cleaning from Monday to Friday. She mopped the kitchen and bathrooms daily, collected the dirty clothes, separated them by color, and washed them every Saturday morning.

In the village, Lariba remembered household chores as fun. She had eagerly learned how to cook and clean properly under the watchful eye of her mother, Akurugo. However, with her big sister in the city, chores became more tedious and were routinely inspected by Agnes. The house was spacious, with three bedrooms and three bathrooms, but there was no room designated for Lariba, and she slept on the couch in the living room near the kitchen.

One night, when the house was quiet, Lariba was exhausted and fell asleep on the kitchen floor next to the mop and bucket filled with dirty water. Agnes, like a true taskmaster, woke up in the middle of the night for a routine house inspection and discovered Lariba asleep on the job. Agnes was furious. She quickly grabbed a red belt from Rex's trousers and beat her. Lariba woke up from the blows, pleading for mercy, but her sister continued to strike her in rage.

Meanwhile, Lariba's nephews, Adeno and Yenime, watched television in adjacent rooms, undisturbed by the commotion in the kitchen. After the beating, Lariba remained still on the kitchen floor for a moment, trying to catch her breath. When she finally regained her energy, she picked herself up, emptied the bucket of dirty water, refilled it with warm water, and soaked herself in Epsom salt. Her body was covered in bruises on her arms, legs, and back.

The next morning, after breakfast, Lariba carefully gathered all the dirty clothes in the house, separated them by color, and washed them. She learned never to fall asleep on the job and to complete all her assigned duties in her sister's house. Unfortunately, some of the scars and bruises from the beatings became permanent.

On holidays, Rex would take a break from his political responsibilities and take the family on an excursion. "It's always a surprise and always fun," assured Adeno, Lariba's nephew. This time, the excursion wasn't very far—it was to a huge pond.

Lariba recalled that Rex approved of the adventure, while Baba disapproved of playing in the river, considering it dangerous. "Looks like fun," she thought. Lariba was excited!

CHAPTER 4

REPTILIAN MONSTER

While in the water with the other children, Lariba noticed a strange object in the bushes with huge bulging eyes slowly submerging into the pond. Frantically, Lariba shouted to Adeno and Yenime, "Get out of the water quickly, there is a monster in the water." They laughed and continued playing, doing backflips high in the air into the pond. This reminded Lariba of the "forbidden river" back at the village.

Lariba observed a little girl sitting on what she probably thought was an old, petrified log. The girl sat on the backside of the reptilian monster, tossing pebbles into the pond. The monster did not move, and the girl did not seem nervous or frightened.

Meanwhile, Rex went to his blue pickup truck, pulled out a live chicken, walked to the edge of the pond near the reptilian monster, and flung the live chicken into the pond towards the monster. On cue, the monster opened its mouth wide and caught the chicken in its mouth. The chicken was heard squealing, then silence as the monster chewed, then swallowed. The monster, with its short stubby legs, waddled back into the water and settled among the tall grass, motionless.

Hours had gone by, the sun settled in the sky. The pond was closed to visitors. The family made their way to the exit. "Were you not afraid, Adeno?" Lariba asked her nephew, who had been dangerously close to the monster several times.

"No," he replied. "That was Uncle Romanus, he is an ancestor. He is perfectly harmless. This is his pond. He, along with the other ancestors, allows us to play as long as we provide lunch. Lunch is usually live chicken. We play in the pond while Uncle Romanus and the other ancestors gobble down lunch. Afterwards, Uncle Romanus finds a shady area among the tall grass and sleeps, undisturbed by visitors."

"We have many ancestors here in the pond. This is their pond. We treat them right; they treat us right, and that's all there is to it," remarked Yenime.

"Besides," added Adeno, "I think Uncle Romanus likes you."

"What makes you say that?" Lariba asked.

"Because every time Uncle Romanus turned his head in your direction, he opened his mouth wide with sharp teeth and smiled," replied Yenime.

Lariba had a good time with Yenime and Adeno. It was the first time she was out of the house, and she finally felt like a part of the family, not just a housekeeper.

Rex, in his diplomatic approach, convinced Agnes to allow Lariba to sleep in on Sunday morning. Except for today, Lariba has been in the house mopping and cleaning since she has been here. She deserves a day of rest. She can sleep in this morning and join us to go to church. What do you think, baby?" Half asleep, Agnes agreed.

Before daybreak, Rex nudged Lariba to wake up. "You are going to church with the family today. Get dressed, we are running late."

The family had all put on church clothes, except Lariba. Her clothes came from the village, worn and wrinkled. Adeno and Yenime's clothes were wrinkle-free! No starch or ironing required. Lariba's clothes made in the village were dingy, worn, and tattered. Attending a new church dressed in old clothes was embarrassing.

Lariba had mixed feelings about church after her experience in Cape Coast and Elmina Castle. Even in the village, sermons from Rev. Father Francis Adom were difficult to understand.

Rex and Agnes were active members in the church; he was a deacon, and she served as an usher. Both wore uniforms, starched, and pressed carefully by Lariba. Both Adeno and Yenime were members of the youth choir.

Every third Sunday, the youth choir performed, led by Sister Clarice, a short, dark-skinned lady with a masterful voice. She served as both the church pianist and choir director. The youth choir, under her leadership, was extraordinary; they were often invited to sing at neighboring churches. The youth choir received huge applause whenever they performed.

It was the third Sunday, Lariba's first time at the church. The youth choir sang. Their voices were amazing. When they exited the stage, one boy in the choir winked at Lariba. At first, she was not sure if the boy was winking at her. Lariba had never been winked at before. What did that mean? she wondered.

Lariba felt a strange sensation. She watched the choir boy all the way to his seat, two rows back from her. The boy sat next to an elderly woman with a blue and white wide-brimmed hat. His grandmother or aunt, she thought. The elderly woman elbowed the boy in the arm. Even from a few rows back, Lariba could see the woman whispering her disapproval of his mannish behavior in the house of the Lord. The choir boy was probably a few years older than Lariba. But for some strange reason, he seemed different. Brown-skinned, with a short, well-groomed haircut, and well-dressed with a contagious smile. Every time Lariba and the choir boy made eye contact, he would wink and then smile. Lariba would feel a strange sensation; the sensation seemed to be getting more intense, taking control of her body. Her heart fluttered. Lariba could not help but smile back and wink back.

It was late Sunday night when the family arrived home. Lariba knew she had house chores the next morning. She quickly grabbed her sheet, curled up on the bare floor next to the kitchen, and nodded off to sleep. She was exhausted. Surely, Adeno and Yenime were tired as well. Lariba was anxious to see the choir boy.

The following Saturday, Lariba asked Agnes if she could attend the church service. "We are not going to church tomorrow," Agnes replied. "We are going to the village." Her voice was somber. Villagers and city folks are strangers; they don't always know what the other is thinking.

"How do you feel living here?" Lariba responded.

"I feel okay," Lariba responded.

"We are going to the village tomorrow. Be ready early," she ordered. Lariba was sure her sister was displeased with her housekeeping.

The next morning, Agnes tapped Lariba on the leg to wake her up. She instantly sat up, nervous, wondering if she had done something wrong. "We are going to the village now. It's your friend, Kwame."

"My friend Kwame," smiled Lariba. It had been a while since she had heard anything about her friend.

"He must be feeling better," Lariba said. Then there was an unusually long silence. Agnes cleared her throat. Lariba looked carefully into the eyes of her big sister, searching for clues. Agnes moved closer to Lariba, draped her arm gently over her shoulder, and sighed.

"Kwame's condition has worsened." Lariba was stunned; she was certain his illness was a minor cold. She had no idea he was on his deathbed. Kwame was Lariba's best friend, growing up in the village. They shared many secrets together, including sneaking off in the night and playing in the "forbidden river" and chasing chickens. These two were so close, villagers believed they were blood relatives. Losing Kwame was a devastating blow to Lariba.

By the time they reached the village, it was near nightfall. Lariba slept in her own room, still empty. Her room had been empty all this time. She knew she was being returned to the village. She curled upon the mat and fell asleep. The next morning, Agnes entered the room. She sat next to Lariba and bowed her head.

The room was quiet, so quiet Lariba heard Akurugo and Baba Atuonah breathing in the next room.

Agnes' lips moved to speak, but no words came out. Then she finally said, "Your friend Kwame has gone to be with the ancestors." Lariba's mouth hung open, but no words came out. She was stunned! Her eyes searched the room for understanding. Agnes leaned over and kissed Lariba on the forehead. "I know how much you loved Kwame." Agnes' voice began to break and tremble. Lariba saw her lips tremble. Lariba did not believe what she heard. Lariba refused by keeping her hands folded in defiance in front of her and staring at the floor. She sat staring, wondering, afraid to look up at Agnes. If anyone had asked Lariba to repeat her sister's words, she would not have been able to do so. Lariba covered her eyes with her hands and cried.

The cause of death was "unknown." But Agnes, a registered nurse, suspected it could have been malaria. The symptoms were fever, headache, and joint pain. The next morning, there was a small gathering across the roadside. Villagers and friends, dressed in black, gathered for the funeral service. Rev. Father Francis Adom officiated during the service. Rev. Father Francis Adom spoke eloquently. For the first time, Lariba understood every word. Drums and ceremonial music were heard throughout the village. Kwame's mother, father, and relatives, who had traveled from as far away as Accra, and Kwame's classmates gathered around the shallow grave.

At the conclusion of the service, Rev. Father Francis Adom motioned for a shovel. The family elders lowered a white box into the shallow grave that fitted perfectly for a small boy. In the village tradition, each person emptied dirt into the grave. The shovel was passed from one person to the next, each taking their turn to pour soil into the grave. Once the shovel was handed to Lariba, she froze. Tears streaming down her face, with the shovel shaking in her hand, she poured soil into the hole that contained her best friend. It was an emotional moment for Lariba.

Rev. Father Francis Adom said a closing prayer. All heads were bowed. The grave was packed with soil, patted down with shovels. Lariba stood quietly alone at the gravesite. Already, Lariba was missing her friend. She wondered where he had gone and if she would ever see her friend again.

After the funeral service, food was served: fried rice, jollof, and pito. The symptoms of malaria were pervasive throughout the village. These same symptoms were evident in Baba Atuonah, who had been bedridden for several weeks. Agnes was worried. Lariba saw the fear in her sister's eyes. Across the road was a shallow grave. The earth was freshly turned. The morning was somber.

Lariba excused herself from the service to attend to Baba. His condition had not improved or worsened. He was barely able to muster enough energy to open his eyes and smile as Lariba greeted him cheerfully. "Hello Baba, how are you feeling today?"

She prepared Baba a warm bowl of soup and spoon-fed him, his mouth barely opening. After her efforts, Lariba sat beside Baba gently wiping sweat from his forehead. He was sweating profusely, and his breathing was labored. Agnes took his temperature. Her eyes bulged. She raised Baba up for a cup of ginger tea; he sipped slowly. The pain throughout his frail body was severe. His yellowish eyes told Agnes that Baba had a fever and was also gravely ill.

Baba tried to speak. Lariba saw his lips tremble, but no words came out. After the ginger tea, he dozed off. "I will let you get some rest, Baba." Before she left, Lariba knelt on the room floor, closed her eyes, and prayed. She gently kissed Baba on the forehead. Just before leaving, she turned, glanced at Baba, praying again that he would get better soon. Lariba was fearful that Baba would leave to be with the ancestors before she returned. The door opened, and Agnes stood framed in it. "We will be leaving tomorrow."

The next morning, Agnes, Rex, Adeno, Yenime, and Lariba returned to the city. Lariba sat in the back seat quietly, next to her nephews, staring out of the rear window as they slowly drove away from the village. She reminisced about the good times she spent with her friend and smiled. She thought about the "forbidden river," school days, and chasing the chickens. She wondered about her Baba, who was gravely ill. Would she ever see him again?

Lariba's thoughts shifted to the choir boy. He put a smile on her face and made her happy like Kwame. Happiness is what she needs in her life. Lariba looked forward to seeing the choirboy; his winks, smiles, and swagger in church made her happy. She wondered if she would see him again. With Kwame gone, the choirboy now held a special place in her life. Lariba needed a friend. Once back in the city, it was life as usual for Lariba – cleaning and mopping. On Sundays, with the approval of Rex, Lariba regularly would attend church with the family. She looked forward to church. She looked forward to seeing the choirboy.

.

CHAPTER 5

JADILI

LARIBA SPOTTED THE CHOIRBOY IN CHURCH, and her heart fluttered. He managed to sit in the same row as her, with only one person separating them. Every now and then, the choirboy would lean forward to catch a glance and wink at Lariba. She smiled and winked back.

When it was time for the choir members to go on stage, the choirboy made his way towards Lariba through the center aisle. As he passed in front of her, he paused for a moment to get her attention. "Excuse me, please," he said. She looked up, and they made eye contact. Jadili smiled, and she moved her legs slightly to let him pass. She could feel his body heat as he stood over her, and they once again flirted in the house of the Lord. The choirboy slipped a piece of paper onto Lariba's lap. When she unfolded the paper, she saw a name, Jadili, and his phone number consisting of ten digits.

Outside of house chores and church, school was Lariba's sanctuary. She was now in her senior year at Bolgatanga Senior High School, excelling as an excellent student at the top of her class. She had developed a positive relationship with her academic counselor, who helped her identify suitable colleges based on her interests and talents. Lariba also excelled in track and field, earning numerous accolades, including a partial athletic scholarship.

Living with her sister Agnes and her family, Lariba had outgrown her role as a housekeeper. She aspired to be more than that and had plans to attend college in Accra to study history. Her time with Agnes and her family had taught her valuable skills, and she had developed a particular fondness for the subject of History, inspired by her "end of year" trip to Cape Coast and Elmina Castle.

Agnes and Rex played a significant role in raising Lariba. Under Agnes's watchful eye, Lariba became a meticulous housekeeper, learning how to scrub, wash, mop, and even cook. Agnes often emphasized the importance of cleanliness, saying, "Cleanliness is close to godliness." Lariba understood the metaphor and knew that the condition of a person's kitchen and washrooms reflected the cleanliness of their entire house. Agnes would regularly check the kitchen and washrooms to ensure they were kept clean.

Lariba also became a proficient cook, learning from Akurugo in the village and later from Agnes. She mastered the art of preparing dishes like fufu, jollof rice, banku, and more. During her rare moments of rest, she would think about her dear friend Kwame, their kindred spirit. Even though Kwame had passed away, he would often visit Lariba in her dreams, reminding her of their adventures at the "forbidden river" and their playful encounters with chickens in the compound.

During class, Lariba would often "time travel" in her mind, reminiscing about her time with Kwame. She missed him dearly but also wondered if she would ever see Jadili, the choirboy, again. Lariba remembered that Accra was the capital of a big city, and she hoped for a chance encounter with him when she moved there.

On her first day at Bolgatanga Senior Secondary High School, Lariba went to the main office, where she was pleasantly surprised to hear a familiar voice saying, "Hello." Looking up, she saw Jadili with his infectious smile, as he was a student aide in the main office. He asked if she had her schedule, and when she said no, he offered to escort her to see her counselor. Jadili became her daily personal escort to class, and during their walks together, Lariba discovered that he was polite, respectful, and funny. She was captivated by his handsome face, beautiful smile, and amazing voice. Sometimes, during lunch breaks, they would skip eating and walk hand in hand around the track while Jadili sang in his silky tone. It was a romantic moment for both of them, and Lariba felt a strong connection with him. They had a few secret getaways, including visits to the "forbidden river," where they had fun together. Lariba felt special and a sense of belonging when she was with Jadili. Before meeting him, she had been emotionally and socially challenged, but Jadili provided her with affection and helped her develop into a responsible young adult. Their bond felt unbreakable.

Back in the village, Baba had recovered and resumed farming and tending to the animals. Akurugo continued to take care of Baba, maintain cleanliness in the house, and sell food by the roadside. Lariba made a promise to visit the village twice a year to see Akurugo, Baba, and her siblings. She never forgot the good times she had with Kwame at the "forbidden river," and she felt his kindred spirit whenever she visited the village and stood over his grave, reminiscing, and smiling. Their bond remained inseparable, even in life and death.

After graduating from high school, Lariba moved to Accra to attend Ghana University. Instead of living on campus, she chose to stay with her older brother Bernard and his wife, Nana, to save money and focus on her studies. However, Lariba unknowingly walked into a family feud. Bernard and Nana had a troubled marriage, and their constant arguments made it an unsuitable environment for studying. Lariba felt that Nana resented her, and she would be the target of Nana's frustration whenever they argued. When Bernard would leave the house during heated arguments, Nana would lock the front door and not allow Lariba inside. Without sufficient income, Lariba struggled to secure decent food or housing, especially since Bernard had disappeared. She lived in poor and unsanitary conditions, which affected her hygiene and health. She felt helpless and unable to take care of herself, in terms of basic needs like food, shelter and protection.

CHAPTER 6

HOMELESS

WHEN BERNARD DID NOT COME HOME, Lariba found herself homeless.

Initially, she would curl up outside the apartment door and sleep until Nana discovered her there. Nana's reaction was always intense, screaming and demanding that Lariba leave and return when her brother came back.

Accra's weather was hot and muggy, so Lariba didn't require a blanket. She spent most nights swatting away flies and mosquitoes. To study during the night, she relied on candles in the hallway. During the day, when she didn't have lectures at the university, she would hawk on the streets to earn some money for food. Lariba's possessions were few, all packed into a polythene bag.

Strangely, despite sleeping on the porch, Lariba didn't feel afraid or threatened. Countless other homeless individuals wandered the streets day and night, providing a sense of solidarity. However, she desperately needed a bath, noticing the unpleasant smell emanating from herself. Lariba observed that many other homeless people faced the same need. They wore old, discarded clothes, with matted hair from lying on the streets without pillows.

Eventually, Lariba decided to change her location and found a more peaceful spot at an elementary school that lacked night security. The gates were unlocked, and sometimes the windows of the classrooms were left open. She would carefully crawl through an open window at night, finding a hiding spot under a desk or in a storage room, hidden from passersby.

After weeks of enduring homelessness, Lariba made the choice to return to Bernard's apartment building, braving Nana's anger and verbal abuse. Street life had toughened her, giving her thick skin. One evening, a young man noticed Lariba sleeping outside his door in the narrow hallway. He greeted her as he entered his apartment, sparking a conversation about her situation.

Curious, the young man asked her name and why she was sleeping outdoors. Lariba introduced herself as Lariba and explained that she stayed with her brother and his wife across the hall. When her brother was not home, she had no choice but to sleep outside. The young man expressed concern and asked about her job and how she managed to eat when her brother wasn't home. Lariba evaded the question and simply replied that she managed.

The young man, named Michael, sympathized with Lariba and began bringing her food, such as jollof rice, plantain, and malt. Eventually, he formally introduced himself and invited her to stay at his place until her brother returned, assuring her that she wouldn't be a bother. Lariba gratefully accepted Michael's offer, recognizing that he was a lifesaver.

Living in unstable conditions had begun to impact Lariba's academic performance. She would often doze off in class due to hunger and exhaustion. Lariba asked Michael about his line of work, and he revealed that he worked as an Assistant Manager at a retail store in the mall. Lariba found solace in Michael's modest one-bedroom apartment, where she had a mattress, a desk lamp for studying, and the couch for sleeping.

One evening, Lariba heard a commotion coming from Bernard and Nana's apartment across the hall. The sound of dishes being thrown and glass breaking filled the air as Bernard and Nana fought once again. Bernard was shouting, asking about Lariba's whereabouts, while Nana vehemently denied knowing where she was and blamed Bernard for neglecting his responsibilities. The situation seemed on the brink of turning physical, leaving Lariba on edge as she listened from her spot on the couch.

Bernard eventually stormed out of the apartment, and Nana yelled for him not to return. Lariba remained frozen, standing in the middle of the floor, feeling the full weight of the tense atmosphere. The darkness enveloped her as she stood in complete silence, trying to steady her own racing heartbeat.

Contemplating the events that led to this moment, Lariba wondered if she could have prevented the fighting by going across the hall. She blamed herself for the turmoil, thinking that her presence had caused the strain in Bernard and Nana's marriage. However, deep down, she knew she was not responsible for their problems. Lariba had come to live with her brother at his invitation, with no intention of causing trouble.

Exhausted from the chaos, Lariba rested her head on her opened textbook and drifted off to sleep. Michael, unaware of the commotion, arrived home to find Lariba peacefully asleep on his bed. Not wanting to disturb her, he quietly took a bath and joined her, falling asleep beside her.

Michael had been kind and supportive from the beginning, with no hidden motives. At first, he didn't see Lariba in a romantic light but felt a sense of purpose and responsibility to help a stranger in need. Their friendship grew as they spent more time together, sharing conversations, dreams, and aspirations.

The next morning, Lariba recounted the previous night's events to Michael, who listened attentively, giving her his undivided attention. After a lengthy discussion, Michael tactfully changed the subject, inquiring about Lariba's studying progress amidst the commotion. She admitted that she hadn't been able to focus much due to the ongoing disruptions and mentioned her upcoming examination. Sensing her need for a quiet place, Michael suggested going to Osikan, a serene location near the ocean, where she could study and enjoy a meal afterward.

Lariba's face lit up with excitement at the prospect of food. She eagerly agreed, and they set off for Osikan. The restaurant they visited offered a picturesque setting, with waves gently caressing the rocks along the shore, and the ocean breeze creating a romantic ambiance. It was the perfect place for Lariba to find solitude, reflect, and seek peace.

As they sat together, Lariba's mind wandered to fond memories of her friend Kwame, the adventures they shared in the "forbidden river," and their mischievous escapades with chickens in the village compound. She even thought of her grammar schoolteacher, Ms. Adongo, who taught her about castles and dungeons. Osikan allowed Lariba to reconnect with her past and find solace in the presence of the Almighty.

The restaurant served delicious food, and Lariba and Michael enjoyed their meal while engaging in heartfelt conversations. They watched as the sun set into the sea, creating a lasting memory for Lariba. With Michael's support and the peaceful environment, she was able to complete her assignments due the next day, feeling a renewed sense of confidence.

Upon returning to Michael's apartment, Lariba hesitated to approach her brother's apartment across the hall. She feared encountering Nana and the inevitable confrontation that would follow. Instead, she patiently waited outside Michael's apartment while he struggled with the door key. Curiosity got the better of her, and she pressed her ear against the door to listen for any signs of activity. Surprisingly, there was silence, and she decided it was best not to knock and risk Nana's wrath. Lariba entered Michael's apartment, where she had been staying for the past two nights.

To Lariba's relief, the following morning brought no sounds of yelling or screaming from Bernard and Nana's apartment. She prepared for school, packing her books and school supplies neatly into the pink and green backpack Michael had bought for her. Lariba felt well-rested and prepared for the day ahead, grateful for Michael's generosity and support.

Michael was a responsible and hardworking man, employed full-time as a retail salesperson at the Accra Mall. Lariba cherished their conversations and felt comfortable being herself around him. Despite the quietness emanating from across the hall, their friendship thrived.

Days passed with no signs of life from Bernard and Nana's apartment. The absence of light beneath their door indicated their absence. Lariba, mustering her courage, decided to knock on their door one morning in the hope of finding her brother. However, there was no response, and the sound of her knocks echoed hollowly, as though the apartment were empty. It later emerged that Bernard and Nana had separated, unaware that Lariba was just across the hall, fearful of causing further trouble.

Although Lariba blamed herself for the break-up, it took time for her to realize she was not guilty. She had unknowingly carried the weight of responsibility, thinking she was the cause of the problems between Bernard and Nana. The mystery of Bernard's whereabouts added to Lariba's feelings of homelessness, despite having a place to stay.

There was no information available about Bernard's new location. Due to privacy laws, the apartment management refused to disclose any details to individuals not listed on the lease agreement. Lariba contacted Agnes to inquire if she had heard from Bernard, but she had no information either. Lariba found herself living with a stranger, Michael, without any romantic ties between them. Despite her attempts to create a sense of belonging, she couldn't shake off the feeling of being alone and afraid.

Yearning for guidance, Lariba's thoughts turned to Jadili, the choirboy. She remembered his wit, protectiveness, and care, longing for his presence in this predicament. In some ways, Jadili and Michael shared similar traits, such as their wit, protectiveness, and intelligence. However, Lariba was romantically involved with Jadili while her relationship with Michael remained purely platonic.

Lariba felt safe and comfortable with Michael. They would often share their daily experiences, with Lariba asking about his day and Michael willingly sharing his stories. Lariba expressed her gratitude by preparing dinner for both of them, showcasing her cooking skills learned from her sister Agnes and mother in the village. Their companionship brought happiness to both of them. Michael enjoyed delicious home-cooked meals, while Lariba found solace in having a roof over her head, a comfortable bed, and a quiet place to study.

With time, Michael and Lariba developed a strong bond, becoming the best of friends. Agnes's teachings had prepared Lariba well for her interactions with others, and Michael's wealth of life experiences enriched her understanding of the world. He took pride in providing for Lariba, ensuring they had groceries and sharing his quick-witted sense of humor to keep her spirits high. Michael's presence brought Lariba peace, allowing her to realize her true academic potential and excel in her studies at the university.

CHAPTER 7

A TIME FOR EVERYTHING

AFTER AN EXHAUSTING AND EXHILARATING afternoon of studying, Lariba received a disturbing phone message. "Lariba, this is your sister, Agnes. Baba is not feeling well. His health has taken a turn for the worse. You must return to the village immediately! Baba is gravely ill. Safe and speedy travels." Lariba was stunned. She hurriedly gathered a few clothes and stuffed them into her backpack before leaving. The bus ride felt like the longest ever, and she couldn't sleep a bit. Finally, she arrived at what felt like familiar surroundings. The bitter leaf tree stood guard over the damp clothes pinned to the clothesline, swaying in the warm gentle breeze while guinea fowls and goats roamed about. Lariba knew she was home. Apart from the occasional crowing rooster, there was a strange deafening silence in the compound. Lariba quickly made her way to Baba's room. The door was partially open, and she quietly entered. Baba was lying motionless on a thin bamboo mat on the floor. His chest faintly moved up and down, indicating that Baba was alive but barely. Several wads of used tissue, a waste basket, and a half-empty bottle of water were near the mat. Baba's breath was shallow, and Lariba noticed a shallow mist rising from his gaping mouth. His head was tilted to the side, and his body had stiffened. Lariba stood there, tears streaming down her face. The inevitable had arrived. Baba, after 101 years, had graduated and gone to be with the ancestors.

"He lived a good life," Lariba reflected. "Surrounded by a loving and supportive wife, respectful children, and a close-knit village. Regardless of age, it is never a good time to lose a parent." Reverend Father Francis Adom would often say, "There is a time for everything." Lariba leaned forward and gently kissed Baba on the forehead. "Safe travels, Baba," she whispered and quietly left the room.

The funeral was a magnificent celebration. Elders from neighboring villages, family members, friends, and clergy gathered to pay their respects. Lariba had no idea that Baba knew so many people and had touched the lives of so many. As an elder, he was revered and honored, especially during funeral services. African drums filled the air with rhythmic beats while traditional African dancers performed with pulsating energy. The attendees proudly wore colorful African attire, tribal beads, and piercings. It was a vibrant and respectful gathering.

Reverend Father Francis Adom, a longtime friend of Baba, presided over the funeral alongside elders from neighboring mosques. It was a joyous celebration. The food served was delicious, including jollof rice, kenkey, banku with pepper and stew, dried fish, watermelon, yam, diced pineapple, and pito. Baba's burial site was just across the road from

Kwame's grave site, within walking distance.

At the conclusion of the service, all the elders took the shovel and symbolically poured soil onto Baba's grave, saying, "Ashes to ashes, dust to dust," pronounced by Reverend Father Francis Adom.

In the crowd, Lariba caught a glimpse of a familiar face. She rubbed her eyes, blinked, and refocused, but the face had vanished into the crowd. It was probably one of her nephews, Adeno or Yenime, who both knew Baba well. She shrugged it off. However, as the funeral crowd thinned, the familiar face reappeared. This time, Lariba followed the face through the crowd like a detective. The face moved closer, and eventually, it came into full view. Dressed in African apparel, well-groomed, and wearing a gracious smile. The smile was familiar; it had mesmerized her in church. It was the face she had gently caressed in her dreams and the lips she had kissed. It was the choirboy who used to flirt during church services and be reprimanded by the elderly woman sitting beside him for his inappropriate behavior in the "House of the Lord." The boy who had winked and flirted in church now stood before Lariba at her Baba's funeral celebration. Their eyes locked, and they were once again connected, pure pulsating energy as they drew closer. When they reached out for each other, Lariba felt the tantalizing warm sensation throughout her body, the same sensation she had felt in church—Jadili's smile still giving her butterflies. The flame of their connection still burned brightly in Lariba. Her feelings for him had not changed; she still adored him.

"It was Jadili," they both said almost simultaneously.

"This is my village," Lariba responded.

"Did you know the deceased?" Jadili inquired.

Suddenly, there was a tap on Lariba's shoulder. She turned and saw Ms. Adongo, her elementary school teacher whom she hadn't seen since the end-of-year field trip to Cape Coast and Elmina many years ago. "My condolences for the loss of your Baba," Ms. Adongo said. "He was an honorable man and highly respected in the community. It has been a while. Where on earth have you been, girl?"

As Lariba turned around to introduce Jadili to Ms. Adongo, he had disappeared, dashing through the crowd. "I have to catch my ride," he yelled. "We have a lot of catching up to do." Lariba reached into her pocket and felt a ball of crumpled paper. She unfolded it, revealing ten digits and a smiley face. "Call me." Just as unexpectedly as he came back into her life, her childhood sweetheart vanished once again.

In an instant, Lariba's focus shifted from Jadili to her grieving mother. Akurugo grieved alone, quietly. Several days passed before she uttered a single word. "People mourn differently," remarked one of the village elders.

Lariba stayed in the village for another two weeks, cleaning and helping with the cooking for her grieving siblings, who openly expressed their grief. When Lariba finally returned to Accra, she was emotionally drained. Burying her Baba, participating in the elaborate homegoing celebration held in his honor, and tending to her mother and siblings had taken a toll on her.

CHAPTER 8

PLATONIC

MICHAEL GREETED LARIBA AT THE DOOR with a cheerful smile and a warm embrace when she arrived at the apartment. "So good to see you, Lariba," he said. Lariba rested her weary head on his shoulder and sighed. She was exhausted from her trip to the village. They chatted for a bit, with Lariba sharing highlights from her two weeks there, the time spent with her family and friends, and the delicious food they enjoyed together. However, she conveniently omitted the fact that she had run into her childhood sweetheart during her trip.

"I have good news," Michael announced. "I have been promoted. I finally have my own store. I am no longer an assistant manager." Lariba saw this as an opportunity to share some words of wisdom she had learned from reading "The Alchemist" in her literature class. "When you really want something in life, it is because it originated in the soul of the universe; it is your mission," she quoted. Michael nodded in agreement, and Lariba hugged him tighter, overjoyed to hear the good news.

"Since I will be getting a raise, I will be moving into a two-bedroom apartment closer to the job," Michael said. Lariba noticed that he said "I" and not "we," which made her face drop momentarily. She dreaded the thought of going back to the streets, sleeping in a storage room closet or climbing through the window of the elementary school. But then Michael added, "I would like you to come with me. You can be my roommate." Lariba breathed a sigh of relief and confidently replied, "So, when do we move?"

Two weeks went by quickly, and Lariba gathered her belongings, ready to move into the new apartment. She was excited about having more spacc. In preparation for the move, they went to Accra Mall and bought towels, rugs, curtains, pots, pans, and dishes.

"Do you know how to decorate? Can you turn this two-bedroom apartment into a home?" Michael asked. Lariba had learned a lot about cleaning and cooking from her time at Agnes' house as a young girl, but she had never learned about household decorating. She pretended to know and confidently responded, "I can certainly try." Finally, she would have her own space—a room with a bed, desk, lamp, closet space, and her own private bathroom. Lariba kept the apartment spotless and immaculate. Oftentimes, when Michael came home from work or grocery shopping, he would find her sleeping in his bed. Even though she had her own room, she felt comfortable sleeping with Michael in his bed. Michael never complained. He would undress, then stretch out beside her and fall asleep. As time progressed, their relationship remained platonic, with no late-night hanky-panky.

Over time, gradually the feelings between Michael and Lariba began to change. Lariba would worry when he came home later than usual from work, committing his schedule to memory. She felt comfortable when he was home, sharing a good conversation and preferred him to be there with her instead of working late hours. The feeling was mutual, as Michael worried when Lariba came home late from school. Nightfall brought out the worst in some people, and the campus was not particularly safe late at night. There was no campus security, and the campus lacked illuminating lighting. Even when he knew she had a late class, he felt relieved when she was home safe from the unmentionable things that could happen to her in the night.

They developed an emotional attachment, and the physical attraction between them became undeniable, catching them both off guard and neither of them wanted to ignore it.

One evening, Michael surprised Lariba with a beautifully wrapped package. It wasn't for any special occasion, just something small that he hoped would allow Lariba to lounge more comfortably around the house. The package was meticulously wrapped. Lariba had an eye for detail and loved surprises. She carefully unwrapped the package, unsure of what it was at first. But it was pretty.

"What is this, Michael?" she asked.

"It's a nightgown," Michael replied. Lariba had never seen a nightgown before.

"As I passed the Women's Department Store, I noticed a mannequin in the store window dressed in lingerie. I imagined you in the sheer red lace nightgown. Try it on, hope it fits, hope you like it?" Lariba went into her room, closed the door, and quickly undressed. She carefully put on the gown and admired herself in the mirror, turning from side to side. She decided it was pretty and that she looked good in it. Shyly, Lariba walked back into Michael's room, modeling the nightgown.

"Wow," he gasped. "You look amazing!" He motioned for her to turn around a few times to model. Michael patted the bed and gestured for Lariba to come and sit beside him. She didn't hesitate. The ensuing conversation was jovial. Lariba stretched out across the bed, facing down, gazing into Michael's eyes. The moonlight shone brightly through the partly opened curtains. Michael could see that the beautiful lady before him was well-endowed. Your guess is as good as mine! Between the two of them, the night was full of memorable excitement. It was an excitement that transformed what seemed like a platonic relationship into a strong emotional attachment.

Lariba was in her final semester of her senior year. She could finally see the finish line. She thanked God for bringing Michael into her life at such an important time, when she needed his support.

CHAPTER 9

COMMENCEMENT

LARIBA WENT TO THE UNIVERSITY administration building and read the list of names of those scheduled to graduate. She quickly scrolled down and saw her name. "Hallelujah!" she screamed, raising her hands high in the air, thankful to the Lord for grace and mercy. The struggle had been long, but she had endured. Finally, she had made it and was officially a college graduate. Her name was on the list of graduates from the University of Cape Coast, Accra Campus. She shared the good news with Michael.

She spent most of the day in a salon, getting her hair dressed and doing a manicure and pedicure – compliments of Michael. He was mindful, anticipating her every need, and Lariba was happy. Graduation day had arrived, and she was ready. The graduates assembled on the soccer field, all dressed in royal blue and gold graduation gowns, with graduation tassels blowing in the summer breeze. School officials, dignitaries, alumni, family, and friends proudly gathered for the 45th Inaugural Celebration. Akurugo, Agnes, Rex, Adeno, Yenime, and Michael were all in attendance to support Lariba.

As happy as she was, Lariba couldn't help but think about her Baba. Tears of joy rolled down her face when her name was announced over the loudspeaker. She proudly walked across the stage and received her diploma from the chancellor, turning to face the crowd. The bulbs flashed, and the cheers and applause were deafening. Through it all, Lariba somehow managed to make eye contact with her mother in the crowd. Watery eyes and a runny nose told Lariba that Akurugo was both happy and sad. She missed her husband, wishing he could have been there to share in the celebration.

A day to remember! Lariba wished Jadili could see her graduating, to see that awesome smile on his face. She wondered where he was on such a beautiful and joyous occasion. She needed to feel that sensation. The next time Lariba saw Jadili was at a popular basketball court in the neighborhood, not far from the mall. His basketball skills were exceptional, like a panther in sneakers, maneuvering between, around, and through people, gliding, jumping, and shooting. She watched him from the bleachers beyond the fence. Jadili spotted her, winked, dribbled, and threw a behind-the-back pass. She smiled and winked back, feeling that warm sensation.

"I am out," he announced to his teammates in the middle of the game and trotted off the court to the bleachers to sit with Lariba. Even though his body was drenched in sweat, she found his salty lips and cheeks tasted good. The sensation was mounting. His wet shirt clung to his chiseled body, and she could see his muscular build. "Get away from me with that sweaty shirt, it smells awful," she declared. As offensive as the smell was, she felt even more attracted to him.

When he finally pulled off the shirt, Lariba could see his beautiful chocolate body. Without the sweaty shirt, his body fragrance was appealing to her senses. She wanted him desperately. Jadili and Lariba made plans to meet at a local café later that afternoon.

"One more game, Jadili," one of the guys on the court shouted. "One more player, and we will have a full squad." Lariba pleaded for him not to go, but it was too late. He kissed her on the cheek and whispered confidently, "This won't take long." Jadili leaped from the bleachers and dashed back onto the court.

His body was dry, showing no sign of perspiration. He had not warmed up when suddenly, Jadili slipped and fell on his way to an uncontested lay-up. He hollered and winced in pain as he fell face forward onto the asphalt court. Lariba impulsively sprang from the bleachers, ran through the unlocked fence to Jadili's aid, and gently raised his head, cradling him under her arm.

"Are you okay, Jadili?" she asked.

"I am okay," he responded, but Lariba could clearly see that he was in serious pain. He sat up for a moment under his own power. Two ballers, along with Lariba, helped Jadili to his feet. He hobbled to the bleachers, and the pain was evident on his face as he massaged his knee tentatively. Lariba offered him a ride home, but he refused.

"I am okay," he insisted. "Terry will help me to the car." Terry was his younger brother. As he lifted his leg into the car, he shouted, "Call me. We have a lot to talk about." The car slowly drove away.

Lariba sat for a moment, slumped, face cradled in her hands, reflecting on what had just happened. One minute, she was in the bleachers, watching Jadili play basketball for the first time, and the next minute, he was sprawled out on the basketball court, wincing in pain. It was a roller coaster of emotions, her body tingling with sensation, then tensed with fear and nervousness. An addiction, a hunger that mounted every time they were in each other's presence.

After months, Lariba and Jadili reconnected. They decided to meet at a coffee shop the following day. After a warm greeting and a kiss on the cheek, they sat down. Jadili ordered fried rice with fish and malt. Jadili began with casual conversation and then announced, "I have a surprise for you." In a colorful gift bag with tissue paper, Jadili presented Lariba with a pearl necklace and matching pearl earrings, along with strawberry body mist. He stood up behind her, carefully draped the necklace around her neck, and gently kissed her on the cheek. "Happy belated graduation." Lariba was puzzled. She had never mentioned she was a college student. How did he know she had graduated? They had not communicated, not since Baba's funeral, and even then, she did not mention she was a college student.

"So, Ms. Beautiful, now that you are a college graduate, where do you see yourself in three years?"

It was an odd question to ask on their very first date, but Lariba quickly and confidently responded, "In three years, I plan to be married, a homeowner, and own a business." Lariba was a thinker and a meticulous record-keeper. In college, she had developed the habit of keeping a diary where she jotted down her innermost thoughts daily, and she continued this habit after graduation. She mapped out and fine-tuned her short and long-term goals.

"What type of business?" Jadili inquired.

"I want to own a taxi business."

Jadili was impressed with Lariba's quick and matter-of-fact response. "I read 'Think and Grow Rich' by Napoleon and learned a lot," she added. "Including not to procrastinate and stay focused. 'What you think about, you bring about,'" Lariba confidently quoted from the book. "It doesn't take much to get started. Just a good car, a good mechanic, a reliable driver, and auto insurance. 'The journey of a thousand miles begins with a single step,'" she quoted from the Tao. Lariba had a good Eastern Philosophy professor in her senior year of college who expected all of his students to memorize and internalize famous quotations that would guide them through life's many twists and turns. She had a quotation for every situation, and she dazzled Jadili with her brilliance.

However, Jadili was not particularly impressed with her quotations. All he knew was that Lariba had grown into a beautiful woman, with a curvaceous body. He listened intently to her intellectual responses, but often paid more attention to her mature body frame—thick athletic thighs and voluptuous lips. Jadili was less interested in her goals and aspirations and more focused on his own goal, which was spending a warm, cozy evening with Lariba.

"No children?" he asked.

Lariba blushed. She normally had a quick response, but to this question, she had none. She paused, just long enough for Jadili to interject his thoughts.

"All you need is a good man who makes you laugh," Jadili responded. "If he can make you laugh, he can make you happy. Laughter is the quickest way to a woman's heart."

"Wow! That is poetic," Lariba thought. It made real sense and sounded like music to her ears.

"What are your plans for next weekend?" asked Jadili. "You are invited for dinner at my place. I am an excellent cook," he said proudly. "Afterwards, we can listen to some good music and have a glass of red wine or Smirnoff Ice."

Jadili not only had a great smile but was also an excellent conversationalist, very engaging. Lariba did not drink but always had a healthy appetite for good conversation. She gladly accepted his offer without hesitation. She, too, had questions she wanted to ask, none more important than why he was in attendance at her Baba's funeral and how he knew she was a college student and recently graduated. The stage was set for an unforgettable evening with her childhood sweetheart.

CHAPTER 10

DEJA VU

LARIBA WAS EXCITED ABOUT HER DINNER DATE with her childhood sweetheart. They had much to talk about, and she had many questions. How did he manage to attend Baba's funeral in her village? Was it a mere coincidence? And how did he know about her enrollment and graduation from college? Who had informed him? These were the questions Lariba needed answers to.

Wanting the evening to be special, Lariba decided to spice things up a bit. She chose to wear a royal blue, form-fitting evening gown with a low-cut top that showcased her firm figure. The back of the dress revealed her bronze-like skin, adorned with crisscross straps that accentuated her slender waist. With her graceful stride and hips swaying elegantly from side to side, she was a vision of beauty. Lariba completed her ensemble with the pearl necklace and matching earrings that he had bought for her, and a hint of Opium perfume, a gift from Michael on her 22nd birthday. Her hair was styled, and her nails were perfectly manicured and pedicured. She was truly ready for the evening.

Lariba had often dreamt about this moment, a romantic candle-lit dinner with her childhood sweetheart, Jadili. Soft, easy-listening music would set the mood, igniting a warm sensation that would course through her body. The energy between them was palpable. *There is a time for everything*, she recalled her philosophy professor saying, and this was the right time for Lariba and Jadili to truly connect. She possessed a vivid imagination, and this evening would be more than just a figment of her imagination. It would be a real and romantic night, filled with intense emotions shared with her childhood sweetheart.

However, Lariba's vision was abruptly shattered when she received a troubling phone call from her brother Bernard. Akurugo, her mother, was ill, and she needed to return to the village immediately. Lariba couldn't believe it! It felt like déjà vu. Years ago, she had received a similar urgent call from her sister Agnes, and it had been Baba who was sick. That had not been a false alarm, as Baba eventually passed away and joined the ancestors. Lariba couldn't help but wonder how this could happen on such a special night. Frustration overwhelmed her, and she stomped her foot in disbelief.

The perfect evening with the perfect guy would have to be postponed. Lariba hoped that Jadili would understand, so she called him to deliver the bad news. However, to her surprise, he didn't pick up. She tried multiple times before boarding the bus to the village, but he remained unreachable on the very evening they had planned for their dinner date.

Lariba's thoughts shifted to her mother's condition. What could be wrong with Akurugo? She had never been prone to illness and was known for her strength. Pessimistic thoughts consumed Lariba's mind as the bus finally arrived at the terminal. Rex, a family friend, picked her up, and they quickly headed to the village, located just minutes away. Akurugo lay on the same bamboo mat that Baba used to sleep on, snoring. It was the same room where Baba had taken his last breath. Lariba quietly settled beside her mother, providing comfort throughout the night, fearful that Akurugo might pass away without saying goodbye. Akurugo's skin was damp with sweat, and Lariba could feel the moisture through her own pores.

Amidst the worries about her mother's health, Lariba couldn't help but wonder about Jadili's whereabouts. He was notorious for disappearing, and this would be another question she would have to ask when they rescheduled their much-needed dinner. Lariba extended her stay in the village, taking care of Akurugo, while her siblings began to understand the urgency of their responsibilities. They took on Baba's farming duties as Akurugo slowly recovered. The bitter leaf soup she prepared played a contributory role in her mother's fast recovery, although the fever had been real. Lariba remained for a few more days to ensure Akurugo's full recovery.

Upon returning to Accra, Lariba opened the door to her apartment, hoping to see Michael. However, the apartment was empty as he was still at work. She kicked off her sandals and dropped her backpack by the door before heading to the washroom. As she entered, her eyes fell upon a dozen long-stemmed red roses placed on the sink counter. Lariba was left speechless, her mouth hanging open in surprise. The fragrance of the roses filled the washroom, captivating her senses. Just as she leaned in to inhale the aroma, her vibrating cell phone in her backpack interrupted the moment. She hurriedly made her way to the front room, struggling to unzip the backpack.

Breathless, she answered the call, saying, "Hello," on the verge of exhaustion. A familiar voice greeted her at the other end. It was Michael, her heart filled with joy upon hearing his reassuring tone. He welcomed her home and inquired about her trip and her mother's well-being. They agreed to have dinner that evening, and he made no mention of the roses. Lariba couldn't help but wonder whether the roses were from Michael or Jadili. Jadili always seemed to know her whereabouts, but in this instance, she had no clue.

Lariba freshened up and prepared for dinner with Michael, opting to wear the same outfit she had planned to wear for her dinner with Jadili. Michael arrived dressed in a dark blue silk shirt, black tie, black slacks, and Italian dress shoes. The evening was amazing, starting with an all-you-can-eat buffet at a fancy five-star restaurant. They indulged in seafood, salad, jollof, banku, and rice, accompanied by a variety of drinks, including Sprite, Coca-Cola, iced tea, malt, and, of course, red wine. Lariba decided to take a chance and enjoy a glass of wine with her meal. After two glasses, despite having a full stomach, she began to feel tipsy. Uncharacteristically, she felt more outgoing and less reserved due to the alcohol in her system. Encouraged by her relaxed state, she persuaded Michael to dance. Lariba's youthful spirit allowed her to sway to the rhythmic beats of hip-hop music performed by Kanye West, Chris Brown, and Snoop Dogg. They remained on the dance floor until they were drenched in perspiration. Recovering quickly, Lariba expressed her desire for a slow dance. By this point, after her third glass of wine, she was bordering on being drunk, a sensation she had never experienced before.

Michael favored slow jams, with R. Kelly's "I Believe I Can Fly" being his all-time favorite. With utmost respect, he wrapped his arms around Lariba's slender waist and pulled her close. The fragrance of Opium filled the air, creating a hypnotic atmosphere. Michael was skilled in the art of slow dancing, exhibiting grace and rhythm. They remained on the dance floor for a second and final dance, accompanied by Whitney Houston's "I Will Always Love You." Lariba interlaced her fingers around Michael's neck, and as she nestled her head gently on his chest, they locked eyes for a moment. In her heart, she knew that what she had once considered a platonic relationship was nearing its end.

That night, exhausted from the memorable evening, they stretched out on the bed without bothering to undress or remove their shoes. They fell asleep, finding comfort in each other's presence. The night had been magical for Lariba, rekindling a deep connection with Michael. She felt desired, appreciated, and above all, she felt a sense of belonging.

Weeks passed, and everything seemed to be going well between Lariba and Michael. One afternoon, as she arrived home, Lariba found a note stuck underneath her door. The note simply read, "Meet me at the basketball court tomorrow at ten." Instantly, she knew it was from Jadili. Excitement coursed through her spirit as she anticipated their meeting. The next day, after Michael had left for work, Lariba prepared herself to meet Jadili at the basketball court. She wore a short skirt, high-heeled shoes, and a low-cut blouse, adorning herself with the pearl necklace and matching earrings she had planned to wear on their initial date. Sitting dignified in the bleachers, Lariba waited for nearly an hour before recognizing Terry, Jadili's younger brother, who climbed up the bleachers and took a seat beside her.

Terry greeted her, saying, "Greetings Lariba. My brother apologizes for missing the scheduled dinner date."

Curious, Lariba inquired, "Where is he now?" Terry lowered his head in shame and replied, "Jadili is in jail and will soon stand trial on drug trafficking charges." Her eyes widened in shock as she asked, "What happened?"

CHAPTER 11

HARD TIMES

HE WAS IN A TROTRO FILLED WITH PASSENGERS when the police pulled the driver over. All the passengers, including the driver, were ordered out of the trotro. All packages and bags were carefully searched. Jadili was sitting next to an oversized camouflage duffle bag. The officers discovered that the duffle bag was filled with narcotics and large bills near where Jadili was sitting. The officer assumed the duffle bag belonged to Jadili. He was immediately handcuffed, arrested, and taken into custody. "But the bag wasn't his," Terry declared. "I was there when he got on the trotro. He had only one bag when he got on the trotro, and his bag had plantain, rice, and wine, all for the dinner he was to prepare for you that evening. Jadili is in jail facing narcotics charges. Given all circumstantial evidence, he is innocent."

"When is his court date? I want to be there", Lariba insisted. Still, she had a warm spot in her heart for Jadili; she cared deeply and cringed at the thought of him being in a prison cell.

"When I know the court date, I will surely let you know," said Terry. "Jadili will be happy to see you in the courtroom even if in handcuffs. All he ever talks about is you, how much he adores you and how he hopes to marry you one day. What distresses him is the thought that he might never see you again." Lariba was heartbroken, saddened!

Weeks passed, and a note was left underneath Lariba's door. The note provided Lariba with the date, time, and location of the trial. She marked it on her calendar. She was determined to be present at the trial. She needed to see Jadili; he needed to know he was not forgotten, surely not by her.

Lariba was at the courthouse very early in the morning before it opened. When the doors were finally unlocked, she found the assigned courtroom and found a seat in the front row. Moments later, the bailiff arrived along with court security.

"All rise!" The presiding judge, in his dignified black robe, entered the courtroom. Not before Jadili entered the court led by his court-appointed defense attorney.

Jadili combed the courtroom and made eye contact with Lariba. She waved shyly and smiled. Her heart fluttered when he smiled and returned his flirtatious wink. It was almost as though they were oblivious to their surroundings and the seriousness of the pending charges. She squirmed in her seat, feeling a warm sensation throughout her body. Jadili appeared relaxed and confident throughout the proceedings.

The details of the case were read aloud. Jadili's attorney gave his opening statement. He argued that Jadili was innocent, that all the evidence was purely circumstantial, and therefore the charges should be summarily dismissed.

The prosecuting attorney gave his opening statement. He was a veteran skilled attorney. He argued that narcotics were destroying the community and the lives of innocent children, and that drug traffickers could no longer go unpunished. His argument was persuasive, true, and convincing. Drugs and drug trafficking were a growing problem in Accra, especially among children. The court deliberated for less than an hour.

The jury returned with a unanimous decision. "The jurors find Jadili Griffin guilty of drug trafficking. Mr. Jadili, please stand." The judge pronounced the sentence. "Jadili Griffin, you are hereby sentenced to five years in prison for drug trafficking and solicitation. His shoulders slumped, his persona visibly dejected.

"But he is innocent, Your Honour!" a voice shouted from the back of the courtroom. "My brother doesn't use or sell drugs, and he is not a drug trafficker. He is innocent, Your Honour," Terry pleaded desperately. Tears welled in his eyes; he sobbed uncontrollably when the verdict was read.

"The people have spoken. Court dismissed."

Jadili was taken out of the courtroom the same way he entered in handcuffs. Just before he disappeared from view, he turned his head towards Lariba, smiled, and winked one last time. Tears flowed down Lariba's face. She was devastated! Terry consoled Lariba on the bench just outside the courtroom. Years would pass before she would see Jadili's smiling face again.

Prison life was an eye-opener for Jadili: he witnessed riots, stabbings, rapes, and drug deals. The guards monitored but could not stop it. He learned right away that prison was not about rehabilitation but punishment, whether you were innocent or guilty.

While in prison, Jadili managed to avoid drama and prison politics. The elder inmates took an immediate liking to Jadili. They saw him as a soul worth saving. Instinctively, they knew he was not a hardened criminal. Jadili learned quickly in prison that it was the elder inmates and lifers who called the shots; they decided who to revere and who was untouchable. They were the power brokers, and any favors granted came with their blessings. Jadili was untouchable, protected by the elders. He managed to befriend two guys, both from the north region. They spoke the same language and lived in the same area in Accra – Santa Maria, Ebenezer Junction. They bonded, protected one another, and stayed away from what could be interpreted as prison gossip. It was the elders and lifers who decided who to talk to, who to fear, and which prison guards were fair and honest.

Jadili was always warned ahead if there was a riot about to happen, and advised to remain in his cell and not get involved. Jadili listened to the elders and lifers and managed to avoid riots and bloodshed.

In prison, because of his good behavior, he was granted his own cell. Having his own cell protected him from real thugs and career criminals.

Besides playing dominoes, bid whist, and shooting baskets with his friends from time to time, he needed something constructive to occupy his time while serving time in prison.

Jadili decided to go to school and earn a college degree while in prison. The prison college program was non-existent; access to resources was limited. The prison library had a few good books, but they were loaded with inspirational books. "Things Fall Apart" by Chinua Achebe, "Long Walk to Freedom" by Nelson Mandela, and "Native Son" by Richard Wright were among the books Jadili read in prison. Jadili was well-read and articulate; his vocabulary was extensive. He developed a keen interest in history and politics. Few inmates could read beyond the fifth grade, so they relied on him to explain different political views. He quickly earned the nickname "Professor" while in prison.

Although the college program was small, it was accredited. Jadili earned a Bachelor's degree in Political Science in prison. Teaching was his career goal once he got released!

He maintained his sanity and safety while in prison, mostly by minding his own business and reminiscing about the good times with Lariba. His thoughts and actions helped him distance himself from prison politics and drama, allowing him to mellow in his prison cell and focus on Lariba.

Three years went by in the twinkling of an eye. Jadili was scheduled for his first review before the review board. His behavior was exceptional with prison guards, counselors, inmate elders, and members of the parole board. After serving three years in prison, Jadili was granted early parole for good behavior.

When Jadili was paroled, he moved in with his younger brother, Terry, who lived in Santa Maria, Accra. Jadili had his own business before being sent to prison. He had a rented store and sold books and school supplies. However, the store was taken back by the owner because he could not wait five years to collect his rent. At the time, Jadili's brother was going through financial problems. He could not save his brother's store. So Jadili started from scratch.

To earn money, Jadili, ironically, became a trotro driver. Jadili enjoyed driving. To him, driving a trotro in Accra was an adventure. It required quick reflexes and sound decision-making to avoid gaping potholes on too many unpaved roads, crowded with unthinking drivers. There was never a dull moment.

One skinny adolescent, not older than eleven years, somehow always managed to sneak into Jadili's trotro without paying. The boy would ride all day without a real destination. Jadili noticed the boy in his rear-view mirror moving from seat to seat as passengers exited and new passengers boarded. One day, the boy cunningly stooped down between two boarding passengers and claimed a seat in the rear of the trotro. The boy gazed out the window as though he had something on his mind or a real destination. At the next stop, Jadili turned and glared at the boy. 'Young man, come sit up front and keep me company.' The boy looked around pretending he did not know who the driver was talking to.

Jadili raised his voice and sharpened his tone twice before the boy acknowledged he was talking to him. The boy finally got up from his seat and moved to the front seat next to Jadili. Initially, the boy acted reserved and shy, then quickly became talkative. His speech was incoherent and muffled. His English was poor; he was illiterate even in his native tongue – Twi.

Jadili was fluent in both. This boy was a prime prison candidate, uneducated, talkative with no filter. Jadili thought to himself, 'Someday, if this boy did not get a proper education or marketable skill, he would surely wind up behind bars. Who knows if he would get lucky and be protected by the elder inmates and schooled on how to avoid prison politics and the trappings of career criminals? The lifers in prison would gladly recruit him and use him to do their bidding.'

By the end of the conversation, Jadili realized the boy had never been in a classroom nor had any formal education. 'What is your name?' Jadili asked.

"My name is Shardie."

"What kind of name is Shardie?" Jadili chuckled. He decided to call the boy Reshard. The boy started answering to his new name. Sitting next to him in the front seat, Jadili couldn't help but notice Reshard's clothes were tattered. He wore skinny jeans with a polka-dot underwear showing, almost comical since Reshard was already skinny. He wore an oversized sleeveless red and black Chicago Bulls jersey. His sandals had broken straps, his appearance dusty and raggedy.

Reshard enjoyed riding and talking with Jadili all day if he allowed him to do so. He even admired how Jadili interacted with the passengers, always jovial and respectful. Jadili enjoyed making conversation with Reshard; it made the day go by faster. When the time came to eat, Jadili made sure Reshard had what he had, normally banku with pepper and fish.

Jadili was a superb listener, a survival skill he picked up from prison that kept him out of trouble.

He learned that Reshard lived with his mother and sister in a one-bedroom apartment. There was no running water with a compound bath. He never knew his father. His mother had no formal education and could not read nor write. Reshard needed a guiding hand in his life, someone stern but patient, someone versed in the ways of this cruel, unforgiving world. Jadili decided to take on the challenge.

He learned that Reshard really wanted to go to school but did not know when school started nor how to register. To register for school, you needed a parent or guardian and an address. Reshard's mother could neither read nor write, so they could not help. He, his mother, and sister were wanderers; they moved constantly from one one-bedroom apartment to another throughout Accra.

"When I get my own place, you can come stay with me, but you must go to school. No more joy riding on trotro," Jadili insisted in a fatherly tone. 'I do not want you to end up in prison.'

Reshard gave Jadili a curious look and nodded in agreement. Jadili never shared with Reshard that he was a parolee recently released from prison on narcotics charges.

Reshard seemed to like the idea of going to school and living with Jadili. Even as a boy, Reshard knew he needed structure in his life. Every day on the trotro, Reshard talked only about moving in with Jadili.

"Since you like riding trotro, and you like talking as much as I do, I am going to make you my mate-assistant."

"A mate-assistant?" Reshard asked, inquisitively.

"You will help the traders with their foodstuffs: tomatoes, peppers, smoked fish, and plantain, as they are boarding and exiting the trotro. Sometimes, these items are extremely heavy and awkward. Your help will be appreciated. Afterwards, you will wipe down the seats where the traders sat with their bags."

"What about collecting the money?" Reshard asked. Jadili was not comfortable with allowing Reshard to handle money just yet. Passengers could become angry, even violent if their change were to be incorrect. Reshard needed to know mental math, how to calculate in his head.

"What do you think?" he asked Reshard. Reshard was excited! He had a responsibility. He was learning under the watchful eyes of his mentor.

Finally, now I can have a quiet intimate moment with Lariba, Jadili reflected. *'Find out where your loyalty is, and you will surely find where your heart is,'* he recalled one of the inmate elders' saying.

Jadili decided to take Reshard under his wing and serve as his surrogate father, teaching him proper hygiene, mannerisms, and his native tongue – Twi, and how to reverence elders. "It doesn't matter where an elder is in life, you must show that person respect," Jadili preached.

"If you are blessed, one day you too will become an elder, and you do not want a young snotty-nose boy disrespecting you, condescending your intelligence because of your age or the pace of your walk. Either I will teach you, or you will learn from the school of hard knocks," Jadili declared.

He was focused, driving a trotro, and to him, being a surrogate father was a full-time job. Paramount in his daily thoughts was Lariba. He wanted her to be his responsibility. *How long would it take for him to get on his feet, find a stable job, earn enough money, and afford his own place?*

He wanted Lariba to see that he had something solid to offer. He understood that financial stability was an essential component of a lasting and loving relationship. However, it had only been a few months since his release from prison. They hadn't spoken since his parole, and he wondered how much time he had to win her love.

CHAPTER 12

ENCOUNTER

Jadili and Reshard traveled daily to Sowutuom. This morning was pleasant, and the traffic was mild. Reshard sat next to Jadili on the front seat, munching on a bag of groundnuts. On this particular day, Jadili's mind was preoccupied with Lariba when the steering wheel suddenly began to shake violently. Jadili firmly gripped the wheel with both hands, causing Reshard's groundnuts to spill into his lap, nearly hitting his head on the dashboard. Passengers panicked.

"Hold on everyone," Jadili assured his passengers. He had a jovial relationship with all his passengers, and they felt at ease hearing his calming voice.

Jadili tried to regain control of the trotro by pulling over and safely avoiding a collision from behind. However, the wheel was stubborn and pulled the trotro all the way into the open gutter. Women and children started crying, and passengers carefully scrambled to slide the door open. The vehicle had tipped over onto its side.

Climbing out was no easy task, especially for the elderly and young children.

Reshard assisted the women and children in getting out of the trotro. Fortunately, there were no injuries sustained in the accident. Passengers who needed to go to work flagged down another trotro or taxi, while others sat and calmed their nerves after the life-threatening incident. Jadili comforted each one of his passengers.

Jadili was compassionate and consoling. "You alright, anyone hurt?" He had sustained a minor bruise on his chin from hitting the steering wheel.

After Jadili ensured all the passengers were safely out of the trotro, he discovered that he had a flat tire. He went to the trunk and found that there was no spare tire. He signaled for nearby boys to assist in getting the trotro out of the gutter. The boys were successful, and Jadili expressed his gratitude by giving them money for their time and effort.

However, he was now stranded on the roadside without a spare tire. He called his brother, Terry, for help. He provided his location and asked Terry to go and purchase a new tire.

Meanwhile, Jadili and Reshard crossed the street and walked to the nearest service station to refill the groundnuts and malt that had been wasted in the vehicle. The store had no customers at the moment, but the woman behind the counter was busy on her cellphone and eating 'waakye'. She bore a striking resemblance to Lariba, wearing a multicolored dress, twisted hair, and a pleasant smile.

"Yes, can I help you, sir?" she inquired.

"Yes, where are your groundnuts and malt?" Jadili responded.

The woman graciously came from behind the counter, grabbed a basket, and escorted Jadili and Reshard to the aisle where the items were located.

She was beautiful. The woman was tall, dark-skinned, slender, and curvaceous. She reminded him so much of Lariba, except she was taller and had broader hips.

Customers started streaming into the store, leaving Jadili with no opportunity to flash his magical smile. However, he made a mental note of the service station's location and knew he would surely return one day.

Jadili and Reshard dashed back across the street just as Terry arrived with the spare tire. Together, Terry and Jadili quickly replaced the flat tire, and the trotro was fixed, back on the road, picking up passengers.

CHAPTER 13

SERAPHINE

ONE HAZY SATURDAY AFTERNOON, Jadili found himself window-shopping at the Accra Mall when he spotted Seraphine and her friend at the food court.

"Maaha, Eti sen," what would you like for lunch? I am treating," Jadili offered generously.

Gratefully, Seraphine accepted Jadili's kind gesture. She smiled, and her friend joined in as well. "Medaase." Jadili quickly took charge and called the waitress over. Seraphine and her friend modestly ordered burgers and coke. After placing their orders, they proceeded with formal introductions.

"Jadili, this is my friend, Elizabeth. Elizabeth, this is the guy I told you about."

"Girl, he is cute," Elizabeth whispered to Seraphine when Jadili excused himself to use the restroom. "Does he have any friends?" Elizabeth asked in a half-joking manner. Before Seraphine could respond, Jadili returned from the restroom.

Seraphine politely excused herself to use the restroom as well.

Left alone at the table, Jadili and Elizabeth engaged in light conversation. Initially, it was unclear whether Elizabeth was simply making conversation or attempting to connect with Jadili romantically.

"So, you like my friend?" Elizabeth inquired.

"Yes," Jadili responded without hesitation. His swift reply was evidence enough that he was solely interested in Seraphine.

Elizabeth changed the subject of their conversation.

"You do know she has a birthday coming up next week, right?"

"No, I was not aware."

"You should ask her out on a date. She doesn't have a boyfriend," Elizabeth suggested, now playing the role of a matchmaker. Little did she know, in Jadili's mind, the match had already been made weeks ago.

"What would be a good birthday outing?" Jadili asked, seeking advice.

"Seraphine enjoys the outdoors, and she loves good food," Elizabeth replied. Before she could reveal any more secrets, Seraphine returned from the restroom. The three of them had lunch together, and when Jadili finished eating, he excused himself politely.

"Nice meeting you, Elizabeth."

"Nice meeting you too, Jadili."

Jadili pondered over Seraphine's upcoming birthday. He was already making plans, and with Elizabeth's hints, he had the perfect idea. That Monday afternoon, Jadili decided to surprise Seraphine at her workplace.

"Maakye." Seraphine was taken aback by his unexpected visit. "Would you like to have lunch with me this weekend?" he asked, watching her eyes widen.

"This upcoming weekend is actually my birthday," she replied. Jadili pretended to be unaware, maintaining a straight face. Little did Seraphine know that Elizabeth had already tipped him off.

"Yes, of course," she answered without hesitation.

Seraphine had never been on a formal date before, so she felt nervous. "Where are we going?" she inquired.

"It will be a surprise. After all, it's your birthday." Jadili wanted to leave a positive impression on their first official date. Since neither of them had a vehicle, they agreed to meet at Las-Palmas, a popular local restaurant known for its 'waakye', 'fufu', 'omo-tuo-tuo', and palm soup. They also served "Kiss," a drink preferred by women due to its low alcohol content.

AFTER LUNCH, they hailed a taxi and headed to Achimota Zoo. Seraphine was pleasantly surprised. Jadili was hitting all the right notes.

"Since we had a nice lunch, I thought you might want to feed the monkeys, raccoons, and exotic birds," Jadili suggested. Seraphine playfully kissed Jadili on the cheek.

When Jadili dropped Seraphine off at her house, she appeared visibly tired but happy.

"Thank you for the best birthday weekend I have ever had," she expressed with gratitude.

Jadili smiled and returned the friendly gesture, kissing Seraphine on the cheek as she exited the taxi.

"See you tomorrow?"

"Absolutely."

Jadili had not heard from Lariba, and he began to have second thoughts. His interest in her was gradually fading. Meanwhile, Lariba received a note in her mailbox. It read, "I am FREE! Out on parole." Her pulse quickened, and her heart started racing. She felt excitement surge within her once again.

Lariba quickly forgot that she was in an intimate relationship with Michael. He was her priority, not her childhood sweetheart who had recently been released from prison on narcotics charges. However, Lariba was determined to meet Jadili once more.

How did Jadili find out where she lived? They had only been living in the house for a few months. How did he always seem to know her whereabouts?

She wanted to meet with Jadili, not to rekindle their romance, but to let him know that she had moved on with her life. As she prepared to meet Jadili, she suddenly felt a stomach pain and was rushed to the hospital.

After Lariba was discharged from the hospital, she contacted Jadili and informally ended their relationship. Jadili was taken aback. He couldn't understand why she suddenly wanted to break up. Lariba was not forthright about her reasons for discontinuing their relationship. She failed to mention her recent hospitalization due to pregnancy complications. She also failed to mention that she was involved with another man, and they were planning to get married. Lariba attempted to sound positive and cheerful during her farewell speech over the phone, but she continued to experience sharp abdominal pain.

"Thought you fell off the planet," Jadili sarcastically remarked, trying to make light of the fact that Lariba was ending their relationship.

"My life has become complicated, and I won't be able to see you anymore." Before Jadili could inquire about the complications, the phone went silent.

"Hello? Hello?" Lariba ended the call without even saying goodbye. Jadili was left stunned.

CHAPTER 14

DESTINY

EVEN AS A TROTRO DRIVER, Jadili never lost sight of his dream of becoming a teacher one day. However, he knew that he first needed to obtain his teaching credentials and complete his practicum. He searched tirelessly for affordable credential programs, but such opportunities were scarce. He was eager to regain his independence and become a responsible and productive individual. Above all, he longed to have his own apartment to entertain Lariba. With determination, he worked diligently while attending school, driven to finish his studies and fulfill his goal of becoming a schoolteacher.

Eventually, Jadili secured a position as a substitute teacher in a public school. Teaching in a public-school setting presented its challenges, especially when the students were aware that he would only be there temporarily.

Jadili's teaching experience was unlike any other. Students were immediately drawn to him. He possessed a youthful energy, was articulate, and had a natural ability to connect with others and make learning enjoyable. Teaching came effortlessly to him; it was as if he was born to be an educator.

Terry, Jadili's brother, was incredibly hospitable, but he understood that Jadili desired independence and yearned to stand on his own two feet. Jadili needed a place of his own. Time flew by, and three years swiftly passed.

Michael, no longer a store manager at Achimota Mall, had been promoted to regional manager, responsible for overseeing multiple stores throughout the city. This promotion allowed Michael and Lariba to move to East Legon, an upscale neighborhood, where they resided in a newly constructed five-bedroom house. Their romantic relationship had blossomed, and they were seriously contemplating marriage. However, before taking that step, Michael felt it was crucial to familiarize himself with Frafra marriage customs and engagement traditions. He spoke to both his mother and father about his intention to marry, seeking their guidance. Following the Frafra traditions, an elder from Michael's family, accompanied by a few young men, brought three smoked guinea fowls, kola nuts, tobacco, and drinks to Lariba's family as a symbolic gesture, requesting her hand in marriage.

In the Frafra customary belief system known as "Buuhe," a woman is not considered married even after the marriage ceremony until the man performs certain rites, including the "nu' uhe gme'gme" ritual. As part of this ritual, a big cock and kola nuts are exchanged to seal the marriage. In accordance with Frafra customs, Michael's family presented a big cock, kola nuts, and drinks to Lariba's family. According to their customs, Lariba and Michael were now officially married.

Lariba successfully completed her second *Master's Degree in History* and was overjoyed to be expecting twins. Embracing the prospect of motherhood, she was eager to have children with Jadili. Together, they formed an incredible team, with Lariba helping shape the vision for their family. Michael greatly valued her astute business sense. Lariba often reminded him of Wayne Dyer's motto: "Change the way you look at things, and the things you look at change." By adopting this perspective, they witnessed positive transformations in their lives. Michael considered himself truly blessed to have such an intelligent and insightful soulmate by his side.

CHAPTER 15

TERMINATE

LARIBA SPENT NEARLY A MONTH IN THE HOSPITAL, undergoing tests and blood pressure monitoring. The good news was that she was no longer in the emergency maternity ward, which brought relief to both she and Michael. Now, Michael could visit the maternity ward daily after work and stay until visiting hours were over.

Despite the doctor's orders, Michael would bring food and drinks for Lariba. The doctor insisted on keeping her feet elevated, and the bed was adjusted accordingly. Lariba was allowed to walk for 30 minutes a day on the second floor of the maternity ward. The hospital was the best place for her, as at home she was always on the move. Finally, in the final trimester of her pregnancy, she was discharged, and Michael picked her up at the hospital entrance. Both of them felt relieved, and Lariba was eager to go home and sleep in her own bed.

At home, Lariba kept her legs propped up on the couch. Occasionally, she and Michael would take walks around the neighborhood in the evenings. Michael was extremely protective of Lariba, keeping a close watch on her throughout the night and morning hours. Neither of them wanted to know the gender of their twins; they wished for it to be a surprise. Lariba's only prayer was for a safe delivery and two healthy babies. Michael had no preferences as long as the twins were healthy and resembled him. In an unconventional move, Michael decided that since Lariba was going through all the labor, she should have the first choice in naming the twins, contrary to tradition and custom.

Meanwhile, Jadili and Seraphine were planning their second outing together. Seraphine was not interested in pursuing men for money and lavish dinners; she was a woman of dignity. She knew Jadili was a prideful person who would insist on paying the bill. "Let's go to KFC," she announced, aiming to keep the date inexpensive and affordable.

They ordered fried chicken, coleslaw, mashed potatoes, and fruit juice for two. When they finished eating, Seraphine even insisted on tipping the waiter. Jadili was impressed by Seraphine's kindness. "Now here is a real lady," Jadili thought to himself, recognizing her ability to show appreciation. He made a mental note to pay for their next outing.

During the third trimester of her pregnancy, Lariba was rushed back to the hospital due to severe abdominal pains. She had fully dilated and was immediately taken to the delivery room. Michael remained by her side throughout the ordeal. The moaning, sweating, and screaming were unbearable, even for him. The excruciating pain on Lariba's face horrified him. He had never realized how much pain women endured during childbirth. He did his best to console her, but it pained him to witness his wife suffering. When the first baby was delivered, the pain subsided momentarily, and Lariba returned to normal breathing. However, the labor was not yet over; the midwife awaited the crowning process for the second baby.

Suddenly, complications arose, evident from the expression on the midwife's face. Clumps of dark blood splattered onto the delivery room floor. Lariba's breathing became labored once again. "Push," the midwife insisted. "You still have work to do. You're almost there." Blood continued to flow, and Lariba pushed and strained harder, holding her breath. She anticipated the cry of another baby, but there was no sound of life, only the solemn announcement from the midwife who exhaled, removed the umbilical cord from around the neck of the lifeless soul, and pronounced, "Stillborn."

Lariba remained bedridden in the maternity ward under the doctor's care. Her blood pressure remained elevated.

However, there was still cause for celebration. Lariba had just given birth to a healthy baby boy. Her baby was in the nursery and brought to her occasionally for breastfeeding. After each feeding, her baby would peacefully rest on her breast. His heartbeat was faint, but Lariba was happy. Meanwhile, a birth record was placed on the nightstand next to her bed. Lariba pondered her life, the struggles, sufferings, and disappointments. She thought about the many nights she slept on the streets, homeless, hungry, and afraid. She made a promise to herself that her son would always have a home, enough food to eat, and be surrounded by love, raised by parents who feared God. She wanted her baby to have a special name that embodied strength, protection, kindness, and love. She thought about what gave her confidence and strength during her time living with her sister, Agnes, and what brought a smile to her face.

After a week of mourning, healing, and recovery, a traditional African custom was held to introduce the baby to the world. A brief ceremony was performed for the "outdooring" of the baby. When the baby was brought out for the first time, a small amount of water was poured on the rooftop, and the baby was placed beneath it to let the water drop onto him. This symbolized the changing seasons of life that he should be ready to embrace. The Abusuapani, a designated elder, dipped his finger in water and dropped it onto the baby's tongue, saying, "When you see water, say that it's water." The Abusuapani repeated the same process with alcohol, instructing the baby to say that it's alcohol when he sees it. This gesture was meant to teach the baby to be trustworthy at all times. Following the ceremony, a celebration took place where guests brought gifts such as soap, washing powder, and baby oil.

Lariba decided to name her son Jadili, a childhood name that brought her strength, confidence, and happiness.

CHAPTER 16

BEETS

BEET, SPINACH, AND KALE were recommended by Lariba's nutritionist, along with a lot of clean water, to ensure a fresh supply of breast milk and maintain her own health. Lariba had a desire to have more babies in the future, so she understood the importance of taking care of herself. She realized that childbirth was indeed hard work, which made her prioritize her health.

Her sister, Agnes, was the family's health expert, emphasizing the importance of well-being. "Health is your greatest gift," Agnes would say, a lesson she had learned from studying Eastern Philosophy. When it came to health matters, Agnes possessed knowledge about African herbs, as well as Western and Eastern medicine. Lariba felt motivated to improve her own health, not only for the sake of her baby but also for her husband Michael. She had witnessed her best friend Kwame and her father Baba struggle with health issues that could have been prevented. After her near-fatal childbirth experience, Lariba became determined to be a good mother and, most importantly, to prioritize her own health.

Meanwhile, good fortune had finally come to Jadili. After three long years of intensive studying, he had completed his teaching credentials program and was offered a full-time contract as a teacher at a prestigious private school. Being a teacher had always been his dream, even before his time in prison. It was something he had wanted deeply, worked hard for, and prayed for grace and mercy. He vividly remembered the prophetic words of his dear childhood friend: "When you truly want something in life, it is because it originated in the soul of the universe. It is your mission."

Jadili had built a reputation as a great teacher who made learning enjoyable, and finally, his efforts paid off. He was assigned to teach at Kwame Nkrumah Elementary School in Westland. The students at Kwame Nkrumah adored Jadili and respectfully referred to him as Mr. Griffin. He always had fascinating stories to share, and somehow, he managed to connect those stories to the lessons he taught.

Kwame Nkrumah Elementary School had exceptional leadership, a solid curriculum, and active parental involvement. Whenever the principal gave tours of the campus to guests, he always made sure to visit Jadili's classroom. The students were consistently engaged in learning. During instruction, Jadili would pose thought-provoking questions that encouraged higher-level thinking, and the students eagerly raised their hands to participate. The curriculum was challenging, and homework was assigned at least three times a week. Many parents were delighted to have Jadili as part of the staff at Kwame Nkrumah Elementary.

It was not uncommon for Jadili to invite parents to sit in their child's class or volunteer as parent chaperones on field trips. Jadili had inherited a good school and quickly became one of its most esteemed teachers.

As Jadili entered his fifth year at Kwame Nkrumah Elementary School, a gloomy Saturday afternoon arrived when Seraphine went to visit him. She immediately noticed that he wasn't his usual jovial self, as a grim expression covered his face. Seraphine, familiar with Jadili's moods, could tell that something was wrong. Concerned, she asked, "What's wrong, baby?"

"I have to go to the village next weekend," he responded, his anxiety becoming more evident. "A cloud of grief and sadness is hanging over the village. My spirit tells me that I must return there. Will you please accompany me to the village?"

"Of course, what time should I be ready?" Seraphine replied, offering her support.

Meanwhile, when little Jadili turned five years old, his parents enrolled him in Kwame Nkrumah Elementary School. Just like the other students, little Jadili adored Mr. Griffin. The teacher was always in high spirits and had captivating stories to share. He was delighted when he discovered that the newest member of his kindergarten class shared his name. However, "Jadili" was a tongue-twister and not easily pronounced correctly by the young ones. Instead, Mr. Griffin simply referred to him as "LJ."

Mr. Griffin announced to his class that he would be absent from school for at least a week, leaving the students saddened by the news. LJ had no idea that he would also be absent from school for at least a week due to a trip to the village. When his mother picked him up from school, he noticed her sobbing and asked, "What's wrong, Mommy?"

"I'm okay, baby," she responded, wiping away tears with a handkerchief. Lariba's mother was gravely ill, and it was unlikely she would survive through the night.

The journey to the village began on Friday morning. Lariba spent most of the trip staring out the window. They wouldn't arrive until early Saturday morning, as it took a day to reach Sumbrungo, the village. Unfortunately, before they could reach the village, Akurugo had passed away and gone to be with the ancestors.

CHAPTER 17

TRADITION

A "WAKE KEEP" WAS HELD FOR AKURUGO. People gathered together in the pitch-black impenetrable darkness of night in honor of the deceased. The moonlight served as a flashlight and provided guidance for the village. The next morning, leaf waste and twigs were being burnt. The sky was a hazy gray. As far as the eye could see, there was smoke to repel mosquitoes and flies away from the crowd gathering. Elders spotted in white with a hint of black, signifying the gathering was a celebration.

The deceased was a well-known elder in the village and a respected member of the royal family, with a great history and tradition. This was a gathering not only of members of the nuclear family but also the extended family. The deceased was not only a member of the village but also the entire human family and was celebrated as such. Grudges and misunderstandings were dismissed and forgiven. It was a time of mourning, reflection, love, praise, and celebration. Many of those in attendance were not directly related to the deceased but were invited by a friend. They came to support the family.

The presiding preacher was not always a member of the family but was invited to share the scripture and words of comfort with the family.

Lariba's mother was a member of the royal family, highly regarded, and revered. It was the largest assembly of elders Lariba had ever seen. She had attended many funerals, but nothing like this. Even Michael was amazed at the size of the gathering.

"Who are all these people, Mummy?" LJ asked. "And why are they standing in front of Grandma's apata? I am scared," LJ said as he ducked behind his father, grabbing a hold of his pants leg.

"It's okay," Michael reassured his son. LJ had never been to a funeral.

A huge black awning shaded the casket. People gathered, sitting in neatly arranged chairs. Elders sat separately, draped in royal African garb. When the officiating ended, people danced and praised the Almighty. The swaying to the African dance throughout the celebration signified reverence for the deceased. Tuo-zaafi was served along with fufu, banku, and fish.

LJ immediately calmed down when he saw a familiar face in the distance.

"Look, Mummy, there is my teacher, Mr. Griffin." Lariba turned and looked, and there he was—Jadili. She was shocked. Her childhood sweetheart, handsome as ever! She started to feel that familiar warm sensation all over again. Her hands began to sweat. Her emotions were scrambled. She was shocked, excited, and nervous.

Jadili was not alone. He was standing beside Seraphine, who appeared to be in the early stages of pregnancy. Lariba couldn't wait to talk to Jadili; only this time, she would ask all the right questions, with the intention of getting truthful answers before he disappeared. She wanted to know why he always managed to appear then disappear from her life. Who did he know in her village, a small village where everybody was related? Was he invited to the funeral, or did he know the deceased? These questions Lariba would press Jadili to answer before he, again, disappeared.

"Hello, Eti sen? My son says that you are his teacher." Lariba was probing, looking directly into his dreamy brown eyes. Momentarily, she was distracted and mesmerized by his charming smile.

'Why are you here, Jadili? Were you invited by a friend, or did you know the deceased personally?' A long pause ensued.

'Excuse me, please,' said Lariba. 'Do you mind if I share a word in private with Jadili?' Seraphine politely excused herself so Jadili could talk privately.

'So, Mr. Griffin, why are you here? Did you know the deceased or were you invited? And if you were invited, who invited you?' Lariba bombarded Jadili with a series of straightforward questions.

'Yes, I knew the deceased,' he responded without hesitation.

'She was a member of the royal family.'

Lariba was stunned. Were she and Jadili related? How could she not have known? Her village was small. How could she unknowingly fall romantically in love with a family member? Was this a sin? she wondered. Perhaps the African spirit interfered where they could not have a romantic relationship. But Lariba felt so drawn to Jadili. The romantic urges began to wilt; suddenly, they dried up like raisins in the sun.

She was embarrassed. Lariba did not know her family lineage. She was a marvelous researcher at college but never once thought that the man she fell in love with was her family. "How distant?" she pressed.

"Because your grandmother and my grandfather were siblings. My grandfather, who was your great uncle, left the village when he was a little boy. But he never lost contact with the village lineage and the family. Our grandparents were important figures in the early history of the village. Our lineage was and remains royalty. We are descendants of royalty. You too are royalty, Lariba. We are members of the royal family."

Lariba was dumbfounded.

"My responsibility is and has always been to know the whereabouts of the royal family. That is how I always knew where you were," he explained.

'I knew it,' she thought. Jadili was nothing but a spy snooping in her private affairs, pretending he wanted a romantic relationship. How could she have missed the subtle clues? Lariba recalled when she was a young girl living with her sister, Agnes. Under her repressive restrictions, she was on the verge of being emotionally and socially challenged, but it was Jadili who made her feel special with a sense of belonging. Was she now to believe Jadili was her guardian angel? When he gently embraced her in high school and gave her a gentle kiss on the cheek, in the presence of the entire track team, was this a ploy or a cunning action designed to turn a situation to his own advantage? Even though she felt enlightened by Jadili's explanation and began to see things differently, she could not help but imagine what could have been.

Meanwhile, Seraphine was growing impatient sitting alone amongst strangers waiting for Jadili to finish his lengthy private conversation. Michael was busy eating banku and fish, while LJ was making friends with the other children. Seraphine was seething with anger. After all, she only came at the request of Jadili. She did not come to sit alone and watch him talk to another woman; a woman she was never formally introduced to. She was furious when Jadili gave Lariba a hug.

The soft-spoken Seraphine was boiling with rage but careful not to create a scene. She was at a funeral, a funeral she was invited to by Jadili.

Jadili was having a good time, gleefully engaged in conversation with Lariba. He suddenly realized Seraphine had disappeared. He was bewildered when he saw her racing through the crowd. Where was she running to? he thought. He had driven and had the car keys in his pocket. Lariba's all-important conversation was interrupted as Jadili desperately ran off to catch up with Seraphine. Lariba stood with her mouth open as Jadili chased after Seraphine.

When Jadili finally caught up with Seraphine, she was crouched down next to the car, crying. He knew he had messed up. 'I am sorry, baby, please forgive me.' Jadili begged for her forgiveness for his rude and disrespectful behavior. Seraphine concealed how upset she was, but it was evident from her facial expression and body language she was not happy. Lariba tracked Jadili through the crowd to the parking area. Out of breath, Lariba still wanted to continue the conversation with him.

Jadili's attention was solely on Seraphine. He did not want Seraphine to feel ignored any further. 'We will have to talk later; we still have much to talk about,' Jadili told Lariba as he opened the car door for Seraphine. Seraphine and Lariba exchanged hard glares as the car slowly drove away. A small voice was heard in the distance, 'Goodbye, Mr. Griffin.' LJ was waving goodbye to his favorite teacher.

Michael witnessed the entire drama. He too was puzzled why Lariba was pursuing this strange man and sullen when he drove away.

The car ride back to Accra was unusually quiet. You could hear a pin drop; Seraphine did not utter a single word during the entire trip. The soft-spoken, jovial Seraphine was quiet. She had every right to verbally chastise Jadili for his inexcusable behavior. But she remained cool, calm, and collected throughout the entire trip. Seraphine sat in the car, legs crossed, arms folded, and mouth closed. She spent the entire trip staring out the window, thinking.

Lariba was equally disappointed and frustrated; she had more questions for Jadili. She did learn why there was such an attraction to Jadili; they were family, descendants from royalty, a family of respect and custom.

Jadili was aware of the connection between him and Lariba. All along, he remembered the promise he made to his grandfather before he ascended to the heavens to be with the ancestors. 'Promise me you will take care of Lariba and protect her in any way possible,' was a recurring theme in his dreams. 'I promise to always do my best,' he would say at the close of every prayer. His grandfather had taught him that a real man, like a guardian angel, always keeps his word. And his word to his grandfather was to keep the royal family safe.

Michael knew little about Lariba's family background. He knew she was from the northern region and that her Baba was a proud man and her best friend, Kwame, was her childhood friend. He knew of the traumatic impact on her life when her Baba and best friend left to be with the ancestors. He knew of the warm and loving relationship she had with her mother. He did know of sister Agnes and her domineering and strict house rules.

He did not know Lariba had a romantic crush on a boy named Jadili. He had mixed feelings when he learned that his son was named after a person that she had a romantic connection with.

Even though Lariba came to know Jadili was family with a long and proud history placed in her life for a reason, she never stopped loving him. She felt blessed to know the true meaning of family and honored to be protected and appreciated by two wonderful human beings.

A chapter in her life had closed. She was relieved and grateful she was still alive, loved, and protected. She realized the ups and downs, twists and turns were all part of her life's journey. She felt blessed for all she had received in life. She thanked the Almighty for her husband, Michael, and her son, LJ.

She would never forget Jadili. She had known the true meaning of happiness when they were together. They were royalty.

CHAPTER 18

PREMONITION

"ARE YOU OKAY, BABY?"

Michael asked as he lovingly embraced Lariba from behind. Lariba was wiping away a tear from the corner of her eye, and her nose was running. She reached for her purse to find a handkerchief.

"Yes, Michael, I'm fine. Let's go to the mukyia; I'm starving," Lariba replied.

They interlaced their fingers lovingly and walked gracefully as Lariba loaded her plate with food. She glanced toward the parking area to see if Jadili had left.

Lariba felt enlightened by what she had learned and understood that day. Was she truly of royal lineage? She pondered. Why had her mother never mentioned the name Jadili? Why would Jadili continue to involve himself with Lariba even though they were family? His responsibility was to take care of Lariba and protect her in any way possible. Was Lariba truly happy and secure with Michael? What was Jadili's motive, or was he simply being selfish? Despite these moments of enlightenment, Lariba's attraction to Jadili grew. She couldn't think of anything else as she swallowed a mouthful of banku and fish.

Sitting closely, Michael attentively listened to the rhythm of Lariba's heartbeat. He carefully observed her every movement. When Lariba finished eating and bid farewell to family and friends, the trio—Lariba, LJ, and Michael—walked over to the open grave site. The elders had already taken the designated shovel, and according to tradition, each person shoveled soil into the open grave. At the age of eight, Lariba had lived a full life surrounded by family and love. Now, family and friends in the village where Lariba was born had gathered to bid farewell to an elder, her mother, Akurugo. She was a member of the royal family. Losing a parent, especially one's mother, was never easy. They bowed in silence for a moment of prayer for Akurugo. Lariba picked up the designated shovel and tossed soil into the open grave.

There is a time for everything, Michael thought as they slowly made their way to the car. Everyone, including Michael, was exhausted. They had a long drive ahead, and Michael was the designated driver. He would have to navigate the rough roads at night.

"Who was the person you were talking to at the funeral?" Michael asked in a pleasant yet curious tone. He listened attentively for Lariba's response, but she remained silent. When he looked over, he saw that

Lariba had dozed off and was fast asleep. LJ in the back seat was stretched out, also sound asleep. By the time they arrived home, it was nearly midnight. Lariba was groggy and not in the mood to answer questions. However, Michael was determined to continue his inquiry.

The following morning, Michael asked again, "Who was that person you were talking to at the funeral?"

Lariba shrugged off the question. "Just a family friend," she responded nonchalantly.

"No, Daddy, that was Mr. Griffin, my best and favorite teacher in the whole wide world," LJ interjected.

Michael instantly became more curious. Why hadn't Lariba simply mentioned that it was LJ's teacher from the beginning? What was she hiding? he wondered. Did they have a deeper connection than a family friendship? They had spent an unusual amount of time together at the funeral, and Lariba hadn't formally introduced Jadili to him. Michael's suspicious mind started to race. He decided that on Monday, he would take LJ to school himself and find out the truth firsthand.

CHAPTER 19

TRAGEDY

AS MICHAEL BACKED OUT OF THE DRIVEWAY, simultaneously fastening his seat belt, adjusting his rear-view mirror, and talking to LJ, a speeding truck came out of nowhere and slammed into Michael's red Sudan. The driver's side window shattered upon impact, and the driver's door was smashed in, pinning Michael's leg to the console. The force of the collision nearly caused the Sudan to overturn. LJ, who had just fastened his seat belt moments before the crash, was in the back seat. All of this unfolded in front of Michael's house, in the driveway, as he was taking LJ to school. Michael lost consciousness immediately.

Meanwhile, Lariba had a morning hair appointment and had already left. While sitting under the hairdryer at the salon, she heard news of the accident on the morning broadcast. Lariba immediately recognized her husband's red Sudan and the view of her front lawn and rose garden in the background. In a rush, Lariba snatched the dryer from her head, grabbed her purse and keys, and dashed out the door. It wasn't until she turned on the car radio and heard the morning news reporter mention the neighborhood scene and street where the accident occurred that she realized Michael and LJ were actually in the car at the time of the accident. The news reporter provided vague details about the passengers' injuries, leaving Lariba fearing the worst. Her heart raced, and she entered panic mode. Just as she fastened her seat belt, her cell phone in her purse began to ring. She answered the call, and it was her hairdresser, inquiring about her well-being. Tears streamed down Lariba's face as she spoke incoherently. The hairdresser provided some positive news: "No fatalities, three people involved, including a child; they were all taken to the hospital."

"Thank you, Lord," Lariba sighed in relief. The hairdresser stayed on the line, providing support, until Lariba arrived at the hospital. Hysterical and in tears, Lariba rushed through the doors of the hospital's emergency entrance.

There, she was greeted by a nurse who was aware of the car accident. The nurse provided an update and directed Lariba to where she could find her son and husband. Adrenaline pumping, Lariba had enough energy to sprint down the hall to the nurse's station and obtain the room assignments for her son and husband. They were on the same floor but in separate rooms just across the hall from the nurse's station. LJ was in his room, watching television with a breakfast tray by his bedside and seeming to be in good spirits.

LJ was happy to see his mother, and she hugged and kissed him, assuring him she would be back soon. "I'm just going across the hall to check on your daddy. I'll be back shortly."

"Okay, Mum," he replied as he resumed eating breakfast and watching cartoons.

Michael, on the other hand, appeared visibly injured in his room across the hall. His head was wrapped in white bandages, and blood-soaked bandages were visible in the wastebasket. The curtains were partially drawn, and nurses were attending to him. He was unconscious. When Lariba entered Michael's hospital room, she covered her face, dropped to her knees, and began sobbing.

A nurse helped her to a chair next to her husband's bedside. "Is my husband, okay?" Lariba managed to utter.

"Your husband is fine," the nurse responded. "He has minor bruises, a head injury, and a broken left femur. X-rays will reveal the extent of his injuries in the morning. Visiting hours will be over soon. You are welcome back tomorrow morning. Doctors typically do their rounds at 10 a.m."

Lariba felt exhausted. She kissed Michael on the forehead and whispered, "See you in the morning, my husband." She and LJ left the hospital.

Michael was hospitalized with a broken left femur, bruises, lacerations, and a concussion. Fortunately, the injuries sustained were not life-threatening.

CHAPTER 20

TWO LIVES

SURPRISINGLY, THE NEXT DAY, Michael's first visitor at the hospital was not his wife but Jadili. Michael had just finished his breakfast, and the nurse had taken away his tray when Jadili entered.

Jadili greeted Michael cheerfully. "Bulika."

Michael sat up in his hospital bed, his head cocked with a mixture of anger and indignation and greeted Jadili with a smile. "Akwaaba."

Jadili could sense the suspicion in Michael's voice and the anger on his face. Intuitively, Jadili responded, "I'm here, Michael, because of my sister, Lariba. We have a shared history, going as far back as Sumbrungo. I promised my grandfather, who was also your wife's grandmother's brother, that I would ensure Lariba's safety and well-being.

"Now that Lariba is happily married to a capable provider, a good husband, and a father, I relinquish my responsibilities to you. You are now my brother and friend. We are family in the traditions of the Bruni culture."

Clearing his throat, Michael replied, "Your tradition is only slightly different from ours, but our cultures and practices are more similar than different. We share the same ancestral belief system. Regardless of our geographical locations, we are all one people. Our survival as a community has been achieved by showing respect for tradition and by God's grace. We will continue to survive because our history of revering our elders and our love for the Almighty remains deeply ingrained in our souls and spirits. This has earned us favor with the Almighty. Thank you for looking out for Lariba. She is now my wife, and she is in good hands. You need not worry. I will take responsibility for her well-being from now on."

Michael finally confronted his nemesis, firmly asserting his position with a commanding, no-nonsense voice. He was Lariba's husband.

Jadili forced a smile, stood up, and gracefully walked toward the door. Before disappearing from view, he replied with words of wisdom, "Every man has two lives. The second one begins when he realizes he only has one."

EPILOGUE

JADILI WAS FREE from his purported ancestral obligations and was now preparing to marry Seraphine. Two years had passed before Jadili and Seraphine tied the knot. Seraphine, being Ewe, also followed traditional marriage practices. Jadili had to learn about the Ewe's traditional marriage customs to gain permission from both families and formalize their relationship.

Jadili first informed his family about his intention to marry. A delegation from his house was sent to Seraphine's house to meet her father and mother formally and ask for their daughter's hand in marriage. This process, known as "knocking," was familiar to Jadili.

Upon arrival at Seraphine's house, her parents inquired about the purpose of the visit. After learning the reason, the delegates were asked to leave for about a week while Seraphine's parents considered the matter. Jadili was impatient and worried that Seraphine's parents might disapprove of the marriage proposal. Later, he discovered that the postponement was customary in Ewe marriage culture, as they didn't provide an immediate response to important questions. It also allowed them time to inquire about the man seeking their daughter's hand in marriage.

If Seraphine's family was satisfied and Seraphine herself agreed to the proposal, the groom's delegation would be informed on their second visit that their request had been considered and accepted. As a gesture of appreciation, they would bring a payment called the "knocking fee" in the Ewe language. The groom's delegation would bring gin, soft drinks, and 100 Ghana cedis in cash. Once these items were accepted, the groom's family would begin preparations for the marriage payment, known as "srƆnu" or "tabianu." This payment included other items such as an engagement ring, a holy bible, six half pieces of cloth, six pieces of scarf, a waist bead, and a traditional pant.

If the bride's family accepted the marriage items from the groom's family, the ceremony would take place in the bride's parents' house. After the traditional wedding was performed in Tsito, a town in the Volta region, a church wedding was held in Accra.

The wedding was well-attended, featuring dancing, traditional African attire, and served food and drinks. Among the guests, Jadili was happiest when he spotted a familiar face sitting alone between purple and white chairs adorned with balloons and confetti—a face from his not-so-distant past. When his vision cleared, Jadili's smile widened, and his face lit up like a Christmas tree.

The forever young and beautiful woman sat alone at the back of the church sanctuary. She returned his smile, waved, and blew him a congratulatory kiss. Jadili realized that someone from his past had attended the wedding, and he genuinely felt happy. Jadili respectfully smiled at Michael, who was propped up in a hospital bed.

"When a man embarks on his destiny, he often must change his path," replied Jadili. "I have discovered that there exists within me a soul greater than even I imagined."

"God willing, we shall meet again," murmured Jadili. He then turned, zipped up his black leather jacket, and waved goodbye to Michael as he left the hospital.

GLOSSARY

Abusuapani: Presiding elder over a naming ceremony.

Akwaaba: Welcome.

Baba: Father.

Banku: Ghanaian dish made of fermented corn and cassava served with soup or a pepper sauce with fish.

Bolgatanga: A village in the Upper East Region of Ghana.

Bulika: Good morning.

Buuhe: A customary belief system practiced among the Frafra.

Eti sen: How are you.

Ewe: A language spoken in Togo and Southern Ghana. Ewe is part of a cluster of related languages commonly called Gbe.

Frafra: A tribe in Bolgatanga.

Guinea fowl: A type of bird raised like chicken for consumption.

Knocking: A customary practice of seeking a lady's hand in marriage.

Kukuo: Pot.

Maakye: Good morning.

Maaha: Good afternoon.

Medaase: Thank you.

Mukyia: A three-stone cooking fire.

Nemesis: English – A long-standing rival; an archenemy.

Sumbrungo: A region in the Upper East Region of Ghana

Tabianu: Ewe culture; a groom's marriage payment.

Trotro: Privately-owned minibus shared taxis that travel on fixed routes in Ghana.

Waakye: A local Ghanaian dish made with rice and beans.

www.ingramcontent.com/pod-product-compliance
Lightning Source LLC
Chambersburg PA
CBHW070625310726
48982CB00001B/174

9798990858336